# KING
## OF THE
# Streets

# KING OF THE Streets

by

## C.L. Lowry

Creedom Publishing Company
Philadelphia, Pennsylvania

The Cataloging-in-Publication Data is on file at the Library of
Congress.

Visit the website at:
## www.CreedomPublishing.com

ISBN-13: 978-1-946897-60-2
ISBN-10: 1-946897-60-4

Printed in the United States of America
12 11 10 9 8 7 6 5 4 3

For,

# The Streets

# Prologue
## MARTHA BAE, JAMAICA

Money was flowing in Martha Bae. Tourists were checking out all the attractions and loading up on souvenirs. The families that were arriving from different resorts were tipping the locals generously. The sun shined bright in the sky while its rays warmed the earth.

"It's a hot one todeh," an old man murmured, as he walked down the dirt road.

The humidity made the walk uncomfortable. It left him exhausted and fatigued. He stopped briefly and took a sip of the moringa tea that he whipped up the day prior. The cool beverage quenched his thirst on the steamy summer day. He continued down the road and approached a black taxi that was parked alongside the road. Chronixx was blasting out the stereo, and the taxi driver was inside relaxing. His seat was leaned back and his feet were propped up on the dashboard. The odor of sativa emanated from all four windows as he smoked the strong herb.

"Wah gawn lad," the old man said to the taxi driver.

"Skankin' sweet - everybody wanna feel irie. Forget your troubles and rock with me. You nuh feel how reggae music sweet, yeah-e-yeah. Skankin' sweet - everybody wanna feel irie. Forget your troubles and rock with me. You nuh feel how reggae music sweet, yeah-e-yeah. Skankin' sweet," the driver continued singing along with the music and puffing on his herb.

The old man stood by the car, waiting for a response. The music continued blaring, and the driver never budged. It seemed as if someone turned the dial up on the sun because the heat was becoming a bit unbearable for the man. There was no way he would be able to walk to his destination without passing out on the side of the road. He reached into the taxi and turned off the music.

"Yo old man wah yuh doing?" the driver asked, jumping out his seat and giving a death stare to the old man.

"Sorry to badda yuh but mi need yuh help."

"Wah yuh need? Sum money? Cuz eff dat a wah yuh wa mi nuh get none fi yuh"

"No mi need a ride. Mi haffi guh to wuk but mi cyaa walk inna dis heat."

The driver eyed the old man up and saw he was wearing a uniform from the Bahia resort. "Mi cyaa help yuh. Mi waiting fi a group of people mi drop off fi di rafting excursion mi cyaa lef."

"Yuh just get here an di excursion takes two hours to finish. Yuh ave more dan enough time to mek it back." The old man reached into his pocket and pulled out a hundred dollar bill in U.S. currency. "Dis a fi di ride," the old man said as he slid the money to the driver. The driver's eyes widened, and he quickly snatched the bill.

"Cum pon lets guh," the driver replied. He hopped out of the taxi and threw the old man's bag in the backseat. The old man was correct. The rafting excursion took hours, and the taxi driver would surely be back in time to pick up the group he initially brought over.

The ride to the resort was quiet. There was no small talk, and the radio was never turned back on. The old man just stared out the window at the beauty the island had to offer, and the driver kept his eyes on the road. Occasionally his eyes would glance up at the rearview mirror, and he would look at the old man, but still no words were said. Deep down inside the driver wanted to ask the man why he paid him so much for the short ride but it seemed like the less he knew, the better.

It wasn't long before the taxi pulled up to the front gate of the Bahia resort. Palm trees and beautiful landscape surrounded the four-star resort. A large sculpture was one of the focal points of attention for visitors. They took pictures in front of the sculpture, and some even sat around the base. A large light fixture dangled from the tall ceiling and the lights reflected off the glass flooring. The driver was familiar with the protocol, so he waited for the security guards to approach.

"Wah yuh here for?" one of the guards asked. "Yuh here to pick people up?"

"No man. I'm here to drop off a worker," the driver said, pointing to the back seat.

The guard looked at the old man but didn't recognize him, despite him wearing the uniform shirt. "Wah yuh name sir?" the guard asked, standing outside the passenger door.

"Barrington. Mi name Barrington an mi late fi wuk," the old man replied.

"Why nuh mi seen yuh before?"

"Mi nuh kno."

The guard was a solid man. His large stature made him very intimidating. He made it his business to know every employee, whether current or prior. He took his job seriously, and something didn't sit right with him. The old man had features that stood out. His thick gray beard and long dreadlocks would have easily been remembered. "Let mi si yuh ID card."

The old man put his bag on his lap and began rifling through it, searching for the requested documentation. The guard towered over him, peeking into the bag. He looked at the taxi driver who seemed to be wondering what was taking the man so long to find the ID card.

10

"Hol'aan young man mi tink mi feel it," the old man muttered while his hand was buried in the bag.

The suspicious expression on the guard's face showed that he was becoming skeptical of the old man. He gripped his radio and held it up to his mouth.

"Ay, yo Barrington!" someone yelled from the lobby area of the resort. "Yuh late man yuh shift start thirty minutes ago."

The guard turned and saw his supervisor quickly approaching. A large smile spread across the supervisor's round face as he laid eyes on the old man. His stocky frame and large biceps made him a very intimidating man.

"Yuh kno him boss?" he asked while sticking his radio back in the holster on his belt.

"Yeah."

"Ow yuh doing todeh Reggie?" the old man asked as he carefully exited the taxi. The soothing sound of reggae vibes blasted from the lobby, and the flow of visitors caught his attention.

"Mi gud bredda. Cum pon let's get yuh situated." The old man brushed by the guard and eyed him up. The once confident guard barely made eye contact with the old man and quickly found another task to focus on.

The two men worked their way through the resort until they reached one of the suites. "Dis one all yuh bredda," Reggie stated while handing over a master key card. The old man gave Reggie a thick envelope before sliding the key card through the slot and unlocking the door to the suite. Reggie thumbed through the contents of the envelope, counting a large amount of cash. "Let mi kno eff yuh need nuhting else," Reggie muttered before closing the door and backing into the hallway.

The old man stepped into the king suite and looked around the luxurious room. Between the white marble tile, comfortable sleigh bed and ocean view balcony, he wished his stay was more casual than business. He threw his bag on the bed and began unpacking. He removed several items, which included various uniform shirts and camera equipment. The shirts were for each department in the resort, from a maintenance uniform to a chef outfit. The camera equipment was carefully set up near the balcony. Just as the old man screwed the DSLR camera onto the tripod, there was a knock at the door. The knock was very distinct and had a slight rhythm to it.

The old man walked to the door and saw a manila envelope slide under the door. He looked through the peephole but didn't see anyone standing outside the room. The old man opened the manila envelope and smiled once he saw what it contained. He walked onto the balcony and took a deep breath as the fresh island air filled his lungs. *Paradise*, he thought. Just below the balcony were tourists scattered across the private beach. Clear blue water flowed upon the light sand. Children made sand castles, women were sunbathing, and men were crowding the beach bars. Everyone was enjoying all the beauty that Jamaica had to offer.

The old man drug one of the chairs across the balcony. After sitting down, he put his feet up on the banister and pulled out a cigar. He licked his lips before wrapping them around the Henny White cigar and lighting it. The smoke rolled around his mouth like a fine wine before he exhaled the sweet-smelling smoke. It felt good to decompress for a bit as he flipped through the paperwork from the manila envelope. The old man scanned each sheet, which appeared to be copies of sign-up sheets from an excursion company. The itinerary listed each traveler that signed up for various excursions, their room numbers, times they were scheduled to depart the resort, and the duration of each excursion. The old man puffed his cigar and read each name on the list. "Dailey, Dalton, Daniels, Davis. DAVIS. TREY DAVIS," he muttered while inhaling the soothing smoke.

As the old man continued flipping through the paperwork, he noticed the papers went from the excursion list to blueprints of the suites. He studied the layouts and made himself familiar with the location of the beds, closets, couches, and windows.

The entertainment in the resort was keeping everyone occupied. Families were going back and forth from the beach to the pool area. Resort employees were putting on shows and having dance competitions at the pool. The old man set up his camera equipment on the balcony and began scanning the pool and beach area. The lens he put on the camera had excellent zoom capabilities. Faces could clearly be seen, and the old man was focused on every single face. He immediately spotted the initial guard he made contact with when he was dropped off by the taxi. "He's a fuckin' clown," the old man muttered while watching the guard strut around the pool area.

As the old man continued scanning the pool area and beach, there was another knock at the door. It was the same distinct knock as before. After hearing the knock, he made his way to the door but noticed nothing was slid under the door. Laughter and loud conversation could be heard coming from outside the room. He looked through the peephole to see who was making the noise. He saw a family of five standing in the hallway, waiting to get inside their room that was directly across from the old man's suite. There was a woman, whose dark brown skin tone was on display in her pink one-piece bikini. Her hair was braided and the braids hung down to her round bottom. There was a male with light brown skin and curly hair. He had an athletic body type and a few name tattoos that marked his chest. There were two young boys and an infant with the couple. Based on their features, it was easy to tell the adults had to be their parents.

After the adult male opened the door, the family entered the room. "Make sure you guys grab your goggles because we're going to head over to the pool," he instructed. The old man tried his best to see the faces of the adults, but he couldn't see much through the peephole. He stood by the door listening and occasionally looking through the peephole. Approximately ten minutes passed before the door from across the hall opened again. The old man looked through the peephole once more and watched the male exit the room first. The old man's eyes were immediately drawn toward the male's Corona swim trucks. The beautiful woman followed him out the room with the children. Her bathing suit didn't conceal much of her curvy frame. The family made their way down the hall, toward the pool area.

The old man quickly made his way out of his suite and watched the family continue down the hall. He scanned both sides of the hallway, ensuring the coast was clear before moving toward the family's room. After using the master key card, he gained entry into the large room. There were suitcases all over the floor and clothes spread out throughout the room. He began rummaging through each suitcase, tossing around clothing and shoes. There were no valuables in sight, so he worked his way around the room.

"Where is your shit?" he whispered while going through each drawer.

Once the closet doors swung open, the old man was licking his chops. Since there was nothing in the suitcases, he figured their valuables had to be with the family or in the safe that he was now staring at. He punched in the master code of 0-1-0-1 that was printed on one of the sheets of paper from the manila envelope.

*15*

The door to the safe opened and the old man's eyes lit up. Stacks of cash, jewelry, multiple passports, and other paperwork filled the small box. He grabbed the pile of passports and flipped through each one. There were passports from several different countries, but once opened they all contained the same photos. There were photos of each family member. The names in the passports didn't match either. He grabbed the passports from the United States and scanned the information in each one.

"Trey Davis, Naomi Ikawa-Davis, Trey Davis Jr., Mason Davis, Jace Davis." Behind the U.S. passport, the old man grabbed the French passport. The male's photo was also in the passport, but the name read *Gregory Williamson*. The trend continued as he continued opening each passport.

"Come on baby. Let daddy change your diaper," a deep voice said as the room door opened.

The old man had very little time to react, so he just hugged a corner in the closet. He wasn't expecting anyone to return so suddenly.

"Oh my god, you stink so bad."

The man plopped the baby on the bed and started changing the baby's diaper. Between the loud cries of the baby and him focusing on getting his little one cleaned up, he never noticed the open suitcases that had been ran through. "Boy, you smell like a grown ass man," he said while folding up the diaper. Just as he went to throw it in the trashcan, he discovered that his belongings were removed from his suitcase and spread across the floor. "What the fuck," he blurted out before looking around in a panic.

"Sorry about the mess," the old man said while chuckling.

"Who the fuck are you?" the startled man asked while moving toward the stranger. His fatherly instincts kicked in as her stepped between the intruder and his baby, who was still on the bed. "Is this what you motherfuckers do to your guests?" he asked after noticing the old man's housekeeping uniform.

The old man stood his ground and just smiled. His eyes wandered back and forth from the baby on the bed to the terrified father that did his best to block the old man's view. He threw the stack of passports down at the man's feet and watched as fear covered the man's face.

"What the fuck were you doing in my shit?"

"I was just browsing."

"Well, you have five seconds to get the fuck out of here before I whoop your ass."

"Wow, the infamous Trey Davis gives out warnings now? Back in the day, you would just react. Let me found out you got soft."

Trey was so confused. He didn't know what the old man meant by back in the day. Although curiosity wanted to get the best of him, Trey was ready to make a move. He clenched his fists and began closing the distance between him and the old man. Just as Trey got within arm's reach of the old man, he was now staring down the barrel of a nine-millimeter Springfield XD-M.

"Whoa, come on, man. What the fuck you want? You can take the cash, just get the fuck out of here," Trey pleaded as his aggression quickly faded away.

"I ain't here for that," the old man replied as he pressed the gun against Trey's forehead.

"What the fuck yo. What do you want?"

The old man smiled again.

"Wait a minute. You don't have a fuckin accent. You with the Feds?"

"Di accent ongle use wen necessary, and right now it ain't necessary," he said switching between the Jamaican and American accents.

The old man reached into his pocket, pulled out a card, and flicked it at Trey. "Fuck," Trey yelled out when he looked down and noticed it was a playing card. **THE KING OF CLUBS** to be exact. "So you're here to do the dirty work huh?"

"Dirty work? Naw youngin' I'm here to save the empire."

Trey squinted his eyes as he shot the old man a look of disbelief. It was as if the words he wanted to say refused to escape his mouth. The old man took notice of the sudden gaze and smirked, knowing his identity had been revealed. Fear masked the room and Trey's widened eyes began to water. "It can't be."

"Well, it is youngin'."

"How?"

"Now ain't the time to play catch up. I will at least give you the benefit of doubt. I'll give you ten seconds to give me an explanation. What are you doing here?" the old man asked.

The knot in Trey's throat felt like it was growing by the second. A single tear fell from his left eye and onto the floor. The sound of the baby fussing on the bed didn't seem to bother the two men as they continued staring each other down. The old man was cool and calm, while Trey's nerves were on full display. Once the second in command of Atlanta's most powerful crime organization, Trey was not in control for the first time in his life. Every move he made was similar to playing a game of chess. He had to be at least two steps ahead of his opponents. In this current game, it was *CHECKMATE*. With clenched fists of fury and disparity, Trey lunged toward the old man.

The shots ripped through Trey's t-shirt and flesh. He fell to the ground as blood poured from the four bullet holes that decorated his chest. The silencer on the gun muffled the sound of each shot. The last thing Trey remembered was his screaming child who was clearly startled by the loud thump of his body hitting the ground. He tried rolling over, in hopes of using the foot of the bed to assist him back to his feet. The pain was excruciating, and his chest began tightening. His efforts to move were unsuccessful, seeing as though he hadn't moved an inch. The old man watched as Trey struggled to gasp for air. He couldn't move, and he could barely breathe. His vision slowly blurred out as the old man's shoes stepped toward him. A deep chill ran through his entire body and then sudden darkness.

The baby's shrieking cries became louder as every second passed. The old man stepped over the bloody body on the floor and toward the baby. He looked at the baby boy, who was the spitting image of his father. The baby boy's eyes locked on to the stranger that was towering over him, which only made the cries intensify. It was only a matter of time before someone would stop by the door to check on the wailing baby. The old man raised the gun and pointed it toward the spawn of the man he had just murdered. The slack in the trigger was taken out as his index finger slowly squeezed against it.

*BANG!*

# Chapter 1

*SEVEN MONTHS PRIOR*

The large, luxurious mansion was professionally decorated with black and gold balloons, banners, and various party items. It was Ace's 25th birthday, and he wanted everyone and everything decked out in his two favorite colors. To him, black represented power and gold represented royalty. Seeing as though he was one-fourth of one of the most powerful groups to ever run the streets of Atlanta, it was only fitting that he was fond of the colors. The **STREET KINGS** were bosses in the "A," and everyone knew it. Starting off as small-time drug dealers, they grew into investors and property owners. Ace always talked about how each member of the group was the perfect fit for each other. Christopher "Cashflow" King was the son of an infamous cocaine dealer, Corey King. Cash learned everything about the drug game from his father, despite Corey's efforts to keep his son away from the streets. Cash would constantly beg his father to front him some "work" so that he could deal with his friend, but his dad refused. This never became an issue because Cash's best friend, Trey Davis, found a marijuana connect in Bankhead and the two started selling to students at Clark Atlanta and slowly worked their way into the hood.

After about a year of selling, the duo was bringing in consistent money. Although Cash had the financial backing of his father, he enjoyed spending money he earned. It was all about a sense of pride that many called foolish. He didn't care too much for handouts. His Dodge Charger sat in the driveway, next to a luxurious collection of vehicles from Aston Martins to Lamborghinis. Despite the tantalizing options he had to choose from, the choice was always simple. Cash always drove his car.

He and Trey made a killing for years. They stacked up their drug money and purchased matching iced out chains, gold grills for their mouths and BMW 650s. Cash bought his BMW in black and Trey copped his in white. Whenever you saw one, you definitely saw the other. The two were inseparable. It didn't take long for Cash's cousin, Donovan "Don" King, to link up with the duo.

Don graduated from Clark with a Bachelor's Degree in Business. Along with being the plug for the students that were looking to buy marijuana, Don carefully watched his cousin's progression. Knowing that once he graduated he wouldn't be able to help bring Cash customers, he proposed the duo invest in stocks and real estate. They knew everything about the streets but nothing about investing, so they were hesitant to move forward with Don's proposal. After badgering them for months and finally being able to convince them to get on board with his vision, they gave Don cash every month and allowed him to handle their business affairs. Although Cash's father was a self-made millionaire, he never took the time to legitimize his business. Any property he owned was used as a way to move his product at a larger scale. He was proud of the decisions his son and nephew were making.

Cash slowly walked through the living room. His spiked, red bottom shoes tapped on the marble floors with each step he took. He couldn't help but admire himself while walking parallel to the wall-to-wall mirror. A fitted black suit covered his smooth brown skin. The suit jacket had gold trim around the collar, which matched the gold rose lapel, gold jewelry, and gold Cazal shades. Cash was dressed like a true boss. He headed up the stairs and stood over the balcony, which overlooked the large den area. The guests were all decked out in black and gold attire. They were being entertained by a live band and waited on by a five-star catering company. A large, custom cake was centered in the room, replicating a bottle of Ace of Spades. Cash had dropped a couple of stacks to have that cake designed for the party. Everything met Cash's approval, and he couldn't wait for Ace to see everything.

His friend was turning 25, and that was a big deal to the streets. Most young, black men don't expect to live past the age of 21, so Ace had even more of a reason to celebrate. Three years prior, Cash had celebrated his 25th birthday by flying his crew out to Dubai. He wanted to do the same for this celebration, but Ace wanted to stay local so he could be around his family. The Newton family attended, eager for the festivities to begin. Ace's little cousin, Ramir, held up his glass to honor the man he idolized his entire life. Ramir couldn't wait for the day he would be one of the figureheads in the organization. The caterers glided through the room, which was filled with about three hundred people, as they handed out hors d'oeuvres and glasses of champagne. They were happy to be around the fun crowd and even happier to be in the presence of the Street Kings. Serving a party of this prominence would earn them more in one night than they would make in a month.

Cash entered one of the six bedrooms in the mansion and saw Ace standing in front of a mirror, admiring how fresh he looked. His custom black and gold Versace blazer would surely be the talk of the town, especially because he had the Versace shoes to match. Ace's neck was covered in gold chains and his fingers with rings. The piece that stood out was a gold Cuban link chain with a medallion that was designed as a lion's head. This piece sat in front of the rest. The diamond Rolex watch he was wearing stood out too. He was a very flashy person, and on this night, he was living up to everyone's expectations.

Trey and Don were also in the room, scrolling down their iPhones like two teenage girls. Don was always looking for another property or investment to jump on. He was constantly on his phone monitoring the Bitcoin craze. Hundreds of thoughts ran through his head as he tried to think of all the different moves he was ready to make on behalf of the crew. Don didn't want just to be rich. He wanted to be wealthy. He wanted the type of wealth that would ensure his great-grandchildren didn't have to work. He was a major asset to the crew because no one else was on his level when it came to business. Trey was probably messaging his wife, Naomi, because they just had their third child. She had him on a very tight leash, and whenever he wasn't in her presence, she was on his phone line.

"Let's make a toast," Cash announced as he raised one of the four bottles of Ace of Spades that was on the nightstand. "A toast to our goon, our hitta' and our brother. Ace I love you bro, and I hope you enjoy your night."

"To Ace," Trey and Don said in unison while holding their bottles up.

The four men took swigs of the expensive, brut champagne. Each of them twisted up their faces after consuming the rough beverage. "I just want to thank you guys for allowing me to join the crew. I would do anything for you mu'fuckas'. I would not be here with these blessings if it weren't for y'all. I love y'all." The four took another swig of the champagne and got ready to head down to the party.

As soon as the bedroom door opened, loud cheers erupted from below. Ace stepped out of the room first, dripping in swag. He was very confident and stood at the top of the spiral staircase with his arms raised in the air. The rest of the crew stood behind Ace, allowing him to soak up the moment. *All of this shit is for me*, he thought as he slowly descended the stairs. Once he reached the bottom step, two beautiful women were waiting to lock arms with him and escort him through the party. They were caramel beauties with long black hair. One wore a gold dress and the other a black one. Both of the dresses were fitted and hugged their curves, causing every man in the party to stare. Even some of the women were checking them out. Ace wrapped each arm around the waist of both women and palmed their ass cheeks as he walked through the luxurious event. Two photographers and a videographer followed closely behind, snapping shots of the man of the hour. He made his way over to the center of the party and admired the gigantic cake that was perfect for him. "Damn, this cake is dope as shit," Ace said. He was smiling from ear to ear. The band discreetly finished the tune they were playing, which left the room quiet. Ace grabbed one of the bottles that were placed around the cake and raised it in the air. "I just want to thank every—"

*BOOM!!!*

The front door was rammed in, and a swarm of law enforcement agents rushed into the Buckhead mansion. There were members of the Atlanta Police S.W.A.T. team pushing their way through the crowd, alongside agents from the ATF, DEA, and FBI. They were all focused on the Street Kings. Ace tried to make a run for it, toward the kitchen, but quickly realized some of the caterers now had badges draped around their necks and pistols pointed at him. "Get on your knees," one of them ordered. "NOW!" Ace looked over his shoulder and noticed more agents closing in on him. The room was complete chaos. Guests were being detained, and some were actually fighting the agents. Punches were being thrown, and loud screams filled the air. Ace looked over at the staircase and watched as the other members of his group were being placed in cuffs. He quickly darted for the back door but was tackled after the first few steps he took. As his face was being mushed into the marble tile, the feeling of cold steel being clamped on his wrists sent a slight chill up his spine. The same cold steel was also placed around his ankles. Even though he was now cuffed, one of the members of the S.W.A.T. team continued kneeling on

Ace's back. The pain from the knee in his back was nothing compared to the pain he felt watching his crew being carried away in handcuffs. A total of twenty-three arrests had been made at the party and thousands of dollars in damages to the home. Ace was emotionless and didn't say a word.

"Ace Newton," one of the agents stated as he kneeled over the young man. "You are under arrest for murder, aggravated assault, extortion, racketeering and a slew of other offenses. You have the right to remain silent. Anything you say can and will be used against you in a court of law. You have the right to an attorney. If you cannot afford an attorney, one will be appointed to you free of charge. However, judging from the looks of things, I'm sure you can afford an attorney," he sarcastically said as he checked out the interior of the mansion.

Ace was still silent, and the agents lifted him to his feet. For some, being arrested at your own birthday party would be embarrassing but for Ace, it was expected. He knew this day would eventually come. His eyes locked onto those of his family members as he was escorted through the crowd. Tears flowed down everyone's eyes, except Ace's. Police officers were on the scene trying their best to control the situation, but it started to get out of hand. It had the potential to get dangerous. After squeezing Ace into one of the police wagons, he and members of the crew were taken back to the precinct for processing. There was a lot of chatter in the back of the wagon and Ace watched as some of his goons began to sound like bitches.

"Rule number one, is what?"

"No snitchin'," they all said in unison.

"Right. So keep those lips shut. Nobody say nothin'."

A large knot sat in Ace's stomach as they took the ride to the police station. He noticed Cash, Trey, and Don weren't in the wagon with him. Sweat beads began forming on his forehead, and his nerves were getting the best of him. There was no way he could break now, not in front of the underlings in the organization. Ace was someone they looked up to and if he showed any sign of weakness, they would surely flip on him. His poker face was very intimidating, and his opaque eyes seemed to be looking into the souls of each man in the back of the wagon. Something was not sitting right with him. His crew was very careful with their operations, from dealing to investing. Ace took care of all of the crew's dirty work but was careful with the moves he made as well. Although he knew this day would eventually come, the last thing he ever expected was it being on his 25th birthday.

# Chapter 2

*PRESENT*

An eerie feeling came over Cole Weaver as he stood outside the United States Penitentiary in Atlanta. This was the home of some of the world's most famous gangsters. Whitey Bulger, Vincent Papa, and Al Capone are just a few names of men who took up residence in the medium-security facility. Cole had been an attorney for over ten years but had never represented someone facing the federal charges that were brought against Cash. Cole had beaten plenty of local cases for Cash to the point that the Atlanta Police Department couldn't touch him or his crew, but this was a different beast. This was the federal government. The case had piqued his interest, and he knew winning on a federal level would catapult his career. Every crime organization would have him on their payroll, and he would be the recipient of millions of dollars in service fees. This is one of the reasons he represented members of the Street Kings, besides him being good friends with Don. They both attended Clark Atlanta, and Don helped him locate the perfect building to start his firm. Although they graduated in different years, they were a part of the same circle and always kept in touch. *It's show time,* he thought to himself as he straightened his necktie.

Getting into the facility was a thirty-minute process, which left him standing barefoot with just his dress shirt and slacks. Guards had him remove everything else during the search. He had been patted down, his pockets had been gone through, and groin area had been tapped.

"I'm sure this is how you treat all visitors," Cole barked, knowing the extra hospitality was a way the guards set the tone. He thought about filing a complaint with a supervisor, but he had a feeling it would have been pointless. He knew the guards protected each other, and his complaint would have just been swept under the rug.

After signing in, Cole was escorted to an interview room. Walking down the long halls in complete silence, the guards didn't say a word to him. One led the way, and the other followed behind Cole. He would occasionally glance back at the smug expression on the guard's face. There was an obvious dislike between the men, but this was nothing new to Cole. Depending on which client they represented, attorneys often faced the backlash law enforcement officials can't impose on suspects.

The heavy metal door opened and Cole stepped into the interview room. His eyes immediately locked on to Cash, who was sitting in a tan jumpsuit. He had his handcuffed hands placed on his lap. He was unshaven and appeared to have gained a few pounds. To Cole's recollection, there had never been a time in which Cash didn't have a sharp haircut. He was definitely out of his element. Cole patted him on the back, before taking a seat next to him. Cash didn't bother to look at him. Instead, he continued looking straight ahead.

"Good morning, Mr. Weaver."

"It's morning, but I wouldn't necessarily say it's a good one," Cole shot back, looking across the table at the well-dressed man sitting across from them. His olive complexion, dark hair, and goatee gave him more of an appearance of a Hollywood actor, but the badge that was hanging around his neck let them know exactly who he was.

"I am Special Agent Dillon Miles from the Federal Bureau of Investigations," he said while sliding a business card across the table.

Cole slid the business card over to Cash without even examining it. Cash studied the card, verifying the identity of the man who had requested this unexpected meeting. "Why are we here?" Cole asked. "The next hearing isn't until next month."

Agent Miles let out a deep sigh and opened a thick folder that was in front of him. "Well, I have something I would like for you to take a look at." He pulled out a ten-page document and slid it across the table. "I will need an answer after you read that."

Both Cole and Cash read the bold title, **PLEA AGREEMENT**.

"What the hell is this?" Cash asked.

Cole thumbed through the pages and squinted his eyes as he read the text. The words were unbelievable. Agent Miles carefully watched as Cole examined each line. Sweat beads began to form on his forehead, but the last thing he wanted to do was wipe his forehead and show any signs of nervousness. Instead, he looked over at the clock that was on the wall. Cash had his eyes fixated on Miles. He remembered seeing the agent at the preliminary hearing, alongside the prosecuting attorney. Cash's hands twitched as he refrained from jumping across the table and strangling the agent who had turned his life upside down. *I'm facing thirty years. I got nothing to lose if I choke this motherfucker out.* That thought was quickly interrupted.

"You want my client to plea down to a two-year sentence?'

"That's correct?"

"Why?"

"What do you mean?" Agent Miles asked, confused as to why Cole asked him that.

"Why? Why are you offering us a deal?" Cole continued flipping through the paperwork.

"Because he doesn't have a strong case," Cash inserted. His once stone cold face now displayed a slight grin.

"Oh, we have a case. We are just giving you the opportunity to cooperate with us and admit your involvement with the drug distribution."

Cash burst out laughing. "Drug distribution? What the fuck are you talkin' bout? You know nothing about me."

"I know everything I need to know about you, boy."

"Boy?" Cash stood up and almost dove across the table. The guards grabbed him by his shoulders and sat him back down in the seat. His jaw was clenched so tight it seemed as if the bone would tear rip through his face.

"Hold on. Hold on. Everybody calm the hell down!" Cole yelled. "Get your hands off my client," he ordered the guards who disregarded the order. "Chris he is just trying to bait you because he has no case. He wants to jam you up with a bullshit assault charge." Cole turned to Agent Miles and threw the papers in his direction. "Take that plea deal and shove it up your ass."

"Let me tell you something. We are going to go to trial, and I'm going to have the judge throw the book at you and your crew. You are all going to rot in jail."

34

"If that were the case, then you wouldn't be here right now."

Agent Miles pushed the chair back and stood to his feet. He snatched the papers from the desk and stuffed them into the folder. He didn't want to think about what his colleagues would say. He promised he could get Cash to take the plea, but it was obvious he wouldn't. There was a huge hiccup in the case, and Agent Miles promised it wouldn't happen again. The odds against the Feds were astronomical.

"This is ridiculous. Guards take my client back to his cell. We are done here."

"Before you leave I want to know one thing. We will be paying the rest of your little crew a visit. They will be offered better deals than this, and they will take them. Someone will testify against you, and I will have a front row seat to watch you crumble in court."

"First of all, my whole team is loyal, and no one is going to say shit to you."

"Chris, don't say anything else to Robocop over here." Cole walked over to Agent Miles and sized him up. "I will be contacting all my clients and warning them of your little stunt. We will all see you in court."

Agent Miles laughed. "It's such a shame that you are representing everyone involved in this case, Mr. Weaver. Unfortunately, today is the only day we could conduct interviews. Seeing as though your clients have been all placed in different states, I highly doubt you will be available to sit in on those interviews. See, you can't be in three places at once but the federal government can. I'm sure statements are being signed as we speak."

"You can't do that. That's illegal!" Cole barked, knowing it would be impossible for him to reach the other members of the crew in time. Usually, he had time to plan visits with his clients so that he could book flights but there was no way he would be able to do it now.

"We can and we did," Agent Miles muttered before reaching into the pocket of his suit jacket. He pulled out the item and placed it on the table. "We are coming for you," he whispered to Cash before swinging the door open and walking out.

"Yo, get the fuck back here!" Cash yelled. *Fuck*, he thought. He quickly grabbed the item off the table and gave it to Cole.

"What is this?"

"A message."

"What kind of message?"

"An important one. I need you to do me a favor and contact someone about this."

"Who am I contacting?"

"My girl. She will know what to do. Tell her a federal agent gave this to us. You have to call the rest of my crew. They need to know about this agent."

"Ok, I will." Cole flipped the item over, wondering what the significance is about a playing card.

**THE ACE OF SPADES.**

# Chapter 3

*FAIRTON, NEW JERSEY*

Don sat in his cell, reading the business section of the newspaper. His prison experience was a lot different from the others. Don got lucky and became cellmates with Alfred "Big Al" Domingo, who was a major heroin and coke dealer from New Jersey. He was the head of an emerging Italian mob that covered the New York and New Jersey area. When the two were first acquainted, they didn't say much to each other. Big Al wasn't fond of black men. He looked at them as lazy thugs who were more of workers than bosses. The Feds figured it wouldn't take long for Big Al to get rid of Don just like he did all his former cellmates. However, things didn't go as planned. Don took his time and researched Big Al's organization. He learned how they were the resurrected version of the Italian mob. Just as mobs did in the past, Big Al's organization would extort businesses by forcing them to hire his men for protection. If they didn't pay up, they would watch as their stores were destroyed. On occasions, Big Al would send small crews to perform home invasions and kidnappings. His arrogance led to the F.B.I. intercepting phone call conversations and emails, which linked Big Al to several kidnappings and homicides in the Tristate area. "The Big Apple huh? I'm sure you own that city." Those simple words helped form a bond that would take the hands of God to break. Just like Cash, Big Al knew a lot about the streets but knew very little about investing. During Don's time in prison, he spent hours upon hours teaching Big Al how to flip his money into legal assets, and Big Al told Don all about his Dominican drug connects. Don had no worries in prison because Big Al's crew protected their new ally. He was an asset that would take their organization to the next level.

Don was shocked when he found out he had unexpected visitors. Big Al was pulled from the cell and in walked two federal agents that looked like they were serious. As soon as Don saw the agents, his heart began beating out of his chest. He had a gut feeling that the outcome of the visit wouldn't be good. One was an older, black man and the other was a middle-aged, Puerto Rican woman. Don stood up from his bunk and greeted both of them with a smile and firm handshakes.

Even in prison, he maintained a professional demeanor as if he had just entered a business meeting.

"How you doing brotha'? I am Agent Jones and this is my partner, Federal Agent Cruz. We aren't going to take up too much of your time, but we wanted to pay you a visit to discuss an opportunity that just came up."

"Good morning agents, what would you like to speak about? Obviously, you both know there isn't much I can say to you because I have not been awarded the luxury of contacting my legal representation to make him aware of this visit and from the looks of it, you haven't either."

"Oh we contacted Mr. — um, Mr. — Weaver," Agent Cruz said as she hurriedly flipped through the case file she was holding in her hands.

"I'm sorry, Mr. King but it seems like Mr. Weaver is choosing not to participate in this interview," Agent Jones chimed in.

"Well, did you contact Mr. Ricci?"

"Ricci? Dominic Ricci?" Agent Jones asked. He was confused as to how Don would have even linked up with Dominic Ricci.

"Yes, sir."

"He's a mob attorney. How the hell were you able to retain him? We froze all of your assets."

"He's doing it *pro bono*. So if you don't mind calling him and letting him know you are here. I'm sure he would be more than happy to come by and sit through this interview."

"I don't think that would be necessary. You seem intelligent enough to make a decision in this matter."

"And what matter would that be?"

Agent Cruz removed the small packet from the case file and handed it to Don. He took the papers and flipped through them. As soon as he turned to page three, he broke out in laughter. Both agents looked at each other in confusion. They had never seen someone react in such a manner to a shot at freedom. Agent Jones looked around the cell at Don's belongings. He noticed the law books on the ground, next to his bunk. They had underestimated Don's intelligence. It was clear he was spending his time wisely.

"So what happened?" Don asked, folding the paper in half.

"What do you mean?" Agent Jones asked.

"Something had to go wrong. That's why you came here with this nonsense."

"We are offering you that because we don't believe you were directly involved in the drug distribution and killings. We think it was all on your cousin. He called the shots, and we don't want to see you go down for his actions."

"Does that ever work?"

"Does what ever work?"

"That shit you just tried to kick to me. If you truly believed that I had nothing to do with this, I wouldn't be sitting in this cell for the last two hundred and thirteen days."

"Well, this is your chance to get out this cell and back to work."

"Judging by this document, it seems like I'll be out of here soon enough. I would like to thank you agents for the visit, and I will be sure to inform my attorneys of this sneaky move you tried to pull. Congratulations, your names will be added to the lawsuit I plan on filing against the federal government for the constant violation of my constitutional rights."

The agents had no response to Don's remarks. "We will see you soon Mr. King," Agent Jones muttered before snatching the papers from Don's hands. They both left the cell and watched as Don began writing in a composition book. They didn't say a word until they walked out of the penitentiary.

"What the fuck was that?" Agent Cruz asked.

"I have no idea. Miles and Carson said this shit was going to be easy. Miles told me we would be speaking with a thug that would definitely take the deal. That dude was not the average thug."

"He didn't seem like a thug at all. Why the hell didn't we know that Ricci was representing him?"

"That can't be possible. He can't afford Ricci, and Ricci only does business for the mob."

"Well that can only mean one thing. Don is in bed with the mob."

"That would explain why Big Al hasn't beaten the shit out of him yet. He has done it with all his former cellmates, and one was a guy from his own crew."

"Well, I hope Don knows what he's getting himself into. Once you accept a favor from Big Al, you owe him forever."

"Well, he's a smart guy. I'm sure he'll find out soon enough."

# Chapter 4

*FLORENCE, COLORADO*

Ace quietly sat in the room, with his wrists cuffed to the center of the metal table. He was the strongest out the group, but he appeared broken. Not broken physically, but spiritually his soul had changed. The beast had finally been caged. He spent his months reflecting on his actions and the commitment he made to Cash and the Street Kings. Although Ace was a stone-cold killer, he carried himself with respect and dignity. He had always kept his dirt away from his family, so when they all watched him being escorted out by the police, it was embarrassing. Someone would have to pay for that embarrassment. Dipping in and out of depressive states was the norm for Ace. Usually a loner, the hitman of the Street Kings had no choice but to socialize with the people that surrounded him. If he didn't, he would go crazy.

Ace was in a facility with some of the most ruthless criminals in the country and held his own with no problem. The Feds thought he would cower being out of his element, but little did they know he flourished in the new hostile environment. New connections were made, and the Street Kings now had a reach out to Colorado.

Ace's ears perked up at the sound of dress shoes tapping on the cold, concrete floor. The tapping got louder, and the sound of chatter shortly accompanied the noise. Two agents entered the room and stood on each side of him. Ace didn't budge. His head was down and his eyes focused on the bracelets that were tightly clamped on his wrists. If the cuffs were tightened a few more notches, all circulation to his hands would be cut off. It was fitting for a beast to be tamed and in a cage. The agents had heard about how ruthless Ace was, but they had no idea what he was capable of doing.

There was silence in the room. Ten minutes had ticked off the clock since they entered the room. Finally, the silence was broken as a folder was slammed on the table. They were expecting curiosity to get the best of the young gangster, but he still didn't budge.

"Open it up," one the agents instructed.

Still nothing. Their intimidation tactic was useless, and they had no control over the encounter.

"I said open it up!" the agent barked, sliding the folder toward Ace's hands.

"Fuck you," Ace snarled.

The agent bent over. His lips were an inch away from Ace's ears. "Listen you little punk; I'm not one of those dudes back on the streets that you used to run in Atlanta. I hold your fate in my hands. That envelope contains a plea agreement that you are going to sign."

Ace's teeth were grinding, and his veins were bulging out his neck. If he weren't cuffed, he would have snapped the agent's neck. "FUCK YOU!" he repeated.

"No, fuck you. You see your lawyer didn't bother to come. We called him last week, and he said he is no longer representing you. Your friends have given statements and have implicated you in over a dozen homicides back in Atlanta. I am giving you the opportunity to take a plea. Tell me everything about the drugs you guys distributed. I want to know everything."

Ace looked over at the agent. He studied the man's round, clean-shaven face, blue eyes, bald head and thick eyebrows. "FUCK YOU."

CLINK! CLINK! CLINK! CLINK!

Pain shot through Ace's hands and arms. The ratcheting of the cuffs being tightened was followed up by a loud groan. Ace was so focused on one agent, that he didn't expect the other agent to begin squeezing down on the handcuffs.

"You are going to rot in a cell. We know who you are and we know what you do."

The agent opened the folder and pulled out the small item from the top of the paperwork. He put the item in Ace's grimacing face.

"We know you are the Ace of Spades. This is your signature, right? It was found at over a dozen homicide scenes in Atlanta. You are going to get the death penalty, you bastard." The card was flicked in Ace's face.

"Come on. Let's get the hell out of here. This guy is a waste of time," one of the agents said.

The guards grabbed Ace by each arm and escorted him out the room. He was bent over at the waist, hoping the pain in his wrists would miraculously stop. The shackles restricted his steps and shortened his stride. They marched through the facility until they reached solitary confinement. Ace was finally freed from the restraints and placed in his box.

"Give me a minute," one guard said to another before entering the box and closing the door behind her. "Are you ok?" she asked Ace.

"Yeah I'm cool," he replied, rubbing his wrists to get rid of the indentations the handcuffs made. "Who the hell were they? Detectives?"

"No, they were Feds." She grabbed his left wrist and began massaging his skin. Sade Coleman had been employed as a correctional officer for six years. As soon as Ace was processed in the facility, she became fond of him. It was rare an inmate was shipped to their institution with instructions to keep him isolated from the others. This intrigued her, and she had to know more about him. Once she began giving Ace attention, a relationship was formed. He hadn't been there for a month before she started doing favors for him.

"I need to get in contact with my cousin."

"I can contact him for you."

"This is very important. I need you to do it as soon as possible." He removed a pen from her shirt pocket and wrote a number on the palm of her hand. "Call and ask for Ramir."

"Ok. What do you want me to tell him?"

"Tell him that the Feds came up here questioning me about the Ace of Spades."

"That's it?"

"Yeah. He will know exactly what he will need to do."

"I hope this little plan you have lined up includes me."

"Oh, it does, as long as you don't mind coming down to Atlanta with me."

"I don't mind at all. Now since I'm doing something for you, I need you to do something for me."

"I'll do anything."

Sade reached down and grabbed a handful of Ace's private.

Ace pulled on her uniform and wrapped one hand around her throat as sunk his teeth into her neck. She could feel the strength in his grip, which caused her to become moist. She quickly unbuckled her pants, knowing she didn't have much time before having to leave.

"Make it quick," she whispered as she stroked his penis, which was now exposed.

His fingers roamed around her love area before entering the sweet abyss. He turned her around as he slid into her warm box. The pumps were quick but strong, and she did her best not to moan although she wanted to yell out. The last thing either of them needed was for word to get back that they were having a relationship. Sade bit her lip as she used her fingers to spread her lips, exposing her throbbing clitoris. With each stroke, Ace's balls slapped against her clit, which sent her into a whirlwind of pleasure.

"Whose pussy does this belong to?" Ace asked while stroking and watching her round ass bounce against his pelvic area.

"It's yours, daddy."

She felt his hands travel up her uniform shirt. He palmed her breasts and then pinched her nipples. Sade couldn't help but let out a soft moan. Ace was stimulating her body, hitting all the right spots. He increased the speed of his stroke, causing her legs to weaken. His hands found their way back to her ass. He squeezed her cheeks and spread them apart. "Oh shit, right there baby. Oh yeah, daddy. I love you so much."

That's all Ace needed to hear to reach the point of no return. He dumped a warm load inside his secret lover. His grip loosened and his hands caressed her ass, as the final drops of love left his shaft.

"Oh my God, that was so good. My legs are shaking." She began straightening her uniform before exiting. "I'll be in touch."

Ace pulled up his pants and basked in the little glory he received knowing he had slightly infiltrated the federal prison system. From the moment he laid his eyes on Sade, he knew she would be easy to flip. She made eye contact when he sized her up, his compliments made her blush, and she was always watching him. He knew his reputation preceded him. A boss from Atlanta and a young girl from Colorado, was a match made in heaven for her. Only a month had passed when she made some fraudulent allegation that got Ace thrown in solitary confinement. Once there, she had unlimited access to the man she craved for and their relationship began. Once a day, he got to taste her and all favors were returned. Since then, Sade had fallen in love and did anything Ace asked of her.

∞ ∞ ∞

The loud ringing of the phone woke Ramir from a midday nap. He looked at the number of the incoming call but didn't recognize the 303 area code. *Who the fuck is this?* He sat up while wiping the crust out his eyes. He slid the phone icon up and answered.

"Yo."

"Hello," a female voice sounded on the other end of the phone.

"Who this?" he asked, wondering who was calling him from such a random number.

"Is this Ramir?"

"Who's askin'?"

"I'm Ace's girl."

Ramir held the phone away from his ear and just stared at the screen. His eyebrows were now tilted downward, and his mouth was pushed out. The last time he saw his cousin was at the party that was raided. He hadn't even received a phone call from Ace since that night.

"Ace don't got no fuckin' girl. Who the fuck is this?"

"Listen, my name is Sade and I am Ace's girl. I work in the prison he is being held in. The Feds came by to question him today, and he told me I had to call you."

*This bitch works at the prison. This could be a setup.* Everything had to register. Things didn't seem right at all to Ramir. The pieces to the puzzle weren't matching up. This could have definitely been some type of ploy from the Feds to try to get information on Ace. Ramir remained silent as thoughts ran through his head.

"Ramir, I know this all sounds crazy but it is all true," Sade insisted. The last thing she wanted to do was not relay the message for Ace. He would be infuriated.

"Is my cousin ok?"

"I don't think so. The Feds roughed him up a little, and they said they had evidence on him about some cases in Atlanta."

"What kind of cases?"

"I don't know. One minute they were offering him a plea deal and the next, they were squeezing his handcuffs tighter and waving a card in his face." Sade heard a thumping noise after she made her statement. The sound of a fist punching a wall was all too familiar to her because inmates often punched the wall inside their cells out of frustration or as a way to workout. "Ramir, should Ace be worried?"

Ramir wanted to tell her the truth. He wanted to tell her the streets were no longer theirs and their dealers have all found new distributors. He wanted Ace to know everything that was going on, but he was still skeptical of Sade. "Yeah, he should be worried. What prison is he at anyway?"

"The Federal Penitentiary in Colorado."

"Colorado? What the fuck? Why is he all the way up there?"

"I looked up his file, and it seems because of the crimes he was charged with. They are serious enough to hold him up here."

"Well, what about Cash, Trey, and Don? How are they making out?"

"Who?"

"Cash, Trey, and Don. We all got arrested together, but they are the only three no one has heard from."

"Hold on," Sade whispered. "What are their full names? I will check our inmate database to see when they were processed."

"Christopher and Donovan King. They are cousins. Our homie's name is Trey Davis."

The sound of her fingers slamming on a computer keyboard left Ramir in suspense. His main concern was making sure something tragic didn't happen to Cash, Trey, or Don. His heartbeat boomed through the silence as he waited patiently for an answer. He grabbed the half-smoked blunt he started working on the night prior. The aroma of the sativa filled the air, calming his nerves. *Shit, I know they have some bomb ass tree up in Colorado.* Each puff slowly mellowed out his mood and his thoughts began to align.

"I don't see anyone in our system matching those names."

"What you mean? Where are they?"

"Honestly, they could be anywhere in the country."

"So how the hell am I supposed to find them?"

"I don't know if you would be able to."

"FUCK!" Ramir yelled out. "So you said they offered my cousin a plea deal, what was the deal?"

"I never got a look at the paperwork, but Ace wanted no parts of it."

"What did his lawyer say?"

"Lawyer? He didn't have a lawyer with him?"

"What? Why the fuck not? If the Feds are questioning him, he should have a fuckin' lawyer with him."

"He does have a lawyer, but he is in Atlanta."

"What's his name?"

"I think its Cole or Carl Weaver. Something like that. Ace had me call him when he first got here to let him know where he was."

"Oh yeah, I know him, but why doesn't he have a lawyer from out there, especially since this dude didn't show up for a fuckin' plea deal?"

"Trust me, I have told him to get one from up this way but he has so much faith in this Cole guy."

"Well send me a list of the top lawyers in Colorado, and I'm going to get one. Tell Ace to be on the lookout for a new lawyer."

"I will."

"Oh and another thing, what card did the Feds show him?"

"It was the Ace of Spades. What does it mean?"

"Fuck!" Ramir yelled out. "Listen, I got things to do. Send me that list and the address of the prison."

"Wait, what does it mean?"

"Tell Ace I love him and will see him soon."

"Wait —"

*The call disconnected.*

# Chapter 5

"We can't let these thugs get away," Agent Miles said to his partner. "Trey Davis was the only way we were going to make these charges stick. Without him, all we have is circumstantial evidence."

"This is why we should have gotten him on video or at least a written statement from him. Now we have nothing," Agent Carson said.

"I don't think we ever had anything." Agent Miles pulled out a photograph and slid it over to his right. "He was going to skate on us. He had all these passports on him in Jamaica, and I'm sure we would have never heard from him again."

Agent Carson grabbed the photograph and carefully examined it. There was no question that Trey had a plan up sleeves, and the FBI had no idea what it was. Agent Miles flipped through the thick case files. He had been through them at least fifty times, and surely, he would go through them a few more times. He smacked his palm against his forehead repeatedly. Over the course of nine hours, an iced coffee, and a chocolate frosted donut is all he had consumed as he tried diligently to put together his crumbling case. He was almost sure one of the Street Kings would have taken the plea deal, but they didn't. Not only did they not take the deal, but they also didn't even read it.

"Dillon, you ready?"

"Yeah, let's go."

Both agents walked up to the safe house, which was guarded by two other agents. Agent Miles flashed his badge, and the two were granted access into the single-family rancher. As soon as they entered the home, Naomi Ikawa-Davis was observed rocking her baby to sleep. She was in the living room, sitting on the love seat while her other children slept peacefully on the cozy sectional. She didn't even notice the agents walking in the room, but it didn't matter. Her red, puffy eyes showed that she was still grieving the loss of her husband.

"Mrs. Davis," Agent Carson said in an attempt to get her attention.

She continued rocking in the chair and never acknowledged the two agents hovering over her. They watched as tears began to form and trickle down her round cheeks.

"Mrs. Davis," he repeated, kneeling down in front of her. "We need to talk."

Naomi's eyes were looking into his, but they were empty and lifeless. There was so much pain written on her face. Agent Carson had seen enough. There was no way she would be in any shape to testify. He looked at his partner before standing to his feet.

"Let's go," he whispered to Agent Miles.

"Go where?" he barked. "No, we are going to do what we came here to do."

Agent Miles pushed by Agent Carson and stood in front of Naomi. He pulled out a large manila envelope and dropped it on her lap.

"When you get a chance, look at that paper Mrs. Davis. We need you to fill out a written statement telling us everything you know about the Street Kings."

It was as if two waterfalls had formed inside her eyes and tears were now flowing down her face. "Why? Why are you doing this to me?" she asked.

"Doing what?"

"Haven't I lost enough? What more do you want from me?" Naomi pleaded.

"I want you to help me bring down the Street Kings for what they did to Trey and many other people."

"You were supposed to protect us?" Naomi placed the baby on the couch and slowly opened the envelope.

"We tried to help your family. We provided you all with a safe house in Florida, and somehow you ended up in Jamaica."

She wiped the flow of tears from her eyes with her sleeve, as she began sobbing heavily. "It's my fault. I begged him to go there." After the second wipe, her sleeve was drenched.

"You made it very easy for his killer too. Posting those videos on Instagram and telling everybody exactly where you and your family were going to be staying. You have no one to blame but your—"

"DILLON, CUT IT OUT!" Agent Carson yelled. He stepped between his partner and the weeping widow. "Let's go, now!"

"We aren't going anywhere until she writes a statement. I know she knows the inner workings of the organization, and I want it down on paper. All of it!" he yelled while pointing in Naomi's face.

Although tears still filled her eyes, they began piercing through the soul of the agents.

"I told him not to trust you motherfuckers," she muttered as she began writing on a sheet of paper that was in the envelope.

Her hand was moving a mile a minute and the agents watched carefully as they finally got their written statement. At one point, they looked over at each other, knowing they were finally getting the evidence they needed to take down the Street Kings.

"This is what you wanted. This is all you ever cared about!" she yelled as she threw the papers at them. Naomi picked up her baby and held him tight, staring at the agents in disgust. Agent Miles picked up the papers and carefully scanned each page.

*FUCK YOU! FUCK YOU! FUCK YOU! FUCK YOU!* Those two words were written on every single page, from top to bottom.

Agent Miles' face turned bright red, and steam began blowing out of his ears. He charged at Naomi but was held back by Agent Carson. Naomi didn't budge. She stood her ground, toe to toe with the very men that promised her and Trey protection. Protection that she knew they wouldn't be able to trust. A barrage of papers smacked her in the face. Each sheet she wrote on was thrown back at her.

"Get out!" Agent Miles yelled. "Get the fuck out! Go back to the hole you crawled out of."

"Gladly. I don't need you and this dumb ass safe house. I was fine before you assholes ruined my life."

"Well, we will see how long you and your little family stay alive without us. You know how ruthless the Street Kings are, and you already see what they did to your man. Just so you know, you will receive a subpoena to testify and if you refuse to, you will be arrested."

Agents Miles and Carson left the home, leaving Naomi standing in the living room with her children. She now had to face the consequences of her actions and of Trey's decision to cooperate with the Feds. She was now vulnerable.

# Chapter 6

Cole pulled his Audi A8 into the parking garage on Peachtree Street. Downtown Atlanta was packed as usual. Cars filled the streets as everyone did their best to make it to their office buildings, check out the shops, or check-in to the many hotels. Still frustrated with the tactics used by the Feds, he had work to do in order to make sure Ace and Don wouldn't be compromised. Even if one of them decided to take the deal, it would be more than enough ammo for the Feds to throw the book at Cash and bring down the entire organization. He had four meetings scheduled that needed to be pushed back so that he could meet with Cash's girl.

No spots were available on the ground level, so he headed up through the garage. The sound of tires screeching forced him to look into his side mirror, as soon as he pulled into a spot on the second floor.

A red Chevrolet Camaro pulled up behind his Audi and two men hopped out. The driver of the Camaro ran up to the driver's side of the Audi and tugged on the door handle. Cole instinctively pulled the handle to keep the door shut. The men were playing tug-o-war with the door for about a minute before it flung open. A pistol to the back of his head took the fight out of Cole. He was so focused on the driver's door, that he never noticed the gunman enter his vehicle from the passenger side.

"Listen, guys. My wallet is in my left pocket. Take whatever you want, just don't hurt me," Cole pleaded. He was so scared that he almost pissed himself. He always knew representing criminals would catch up to him one day, but he didn't expect that day to come so soon.

"Shut the fuck up. Don't nobody want your fuckin' money," Ramir barked. "We have a bunch of shit to discuss."

"Like what?"

Ramir signaled for the goon at the driver's door to move, and then he held the gun low to Cole's side. The goon hopped in the Camaro and parked in two spots down from the Audi. The last thing they needed was to draw attention to themselves and give someone driving by a reason to call the cops. Cole was still stuck in the same position, afraid to make a move. His hands were shaking rapidly.

"You know Ace?" Ramir asked, digging the pistol into Cole's side.

"N-N-Newton?" Cole asked, struggling to get the name out.

"Yeah, that's my cousin. I want to know why the Feds were questioning him and you weren't there."

"They set me up. They set us all up. I just found out about the Feds going up there to meet with him."

Ramir dug the pistol deeper into Cole's side. Agony was all over his face as the pain shot through his body. "How the fuck didn't you know about it? Ain't that your fuckin' job?"

"Yes it is, but they are trying to get them to flip on each other."

"So that's why they offered him that deal?"

"He didn't take it did he?"

"I don't know, but what does it matter since he had no fuckin' attorney there with him to review the deal?"

Cole didn't have a response. If Ace took the deal, it would mean he would have to testify against Cash and the rest of the organization. He couldn't let that happen.

"How much are you getting paid?"

"What?"

"How much are you getting paid? You ain't doing your job, and I need to find my cousin a lawyer out in Colorado."

"Listen, you don't have to worry about that. I will appoint some of the attorneys in my firm to represent each of them, and I will also find them attorneys in the states they are in. The next time the F.B.I. pulls a stunt like this, we will be ready for it."

Ramir was satisfied with the response from Cole. Not only did this mean Ace would have two attorneys in his corner but it also saved him from wasting time searching for an attorney when other things needed to be done. Some loose ends needed to be taken care of before the Street Kings ran out of time. He tucked his pistol into his waistband, allowing Cole to relax a bit.

"What the hell happened? Why did the Feds lock us all up but keep only Cash, Don, Trey, and Ace?"

"My guess is just as good as yours. They have their files sealed, so I haven't even been able to take a look at the evidence against them."

"You gon' get them out right?"

"Of course. There's a reason the F.B.I. is doing what they can to offer plea deals to each of them separately. They can't have any solid evidence on —"

"— And what the fuck is up with the money. I tried to take some cash out of Ace's bank account for bail, and the bitch at the bank told me they couldn't give me any money from that account."

"They must have frozen their accounts because of the case."

The car shook as Ramir hammer fisted down on the dashboard. "Man, this shit is fucked up. They got bills to pay and shit man."

"Right now, getting them out is the only concern. I will see what I can do about the accounts," Cole said, thinking about the payments that he was scheduled to receive as well.

Representing the Street Kings made him a millionaire, but he wanted to stay one. If he lost this case, and they got sentenced, the F.B.I. would go after their assets next. They were his number one clients and losing them would be a loss of approximately sixty percent of his income.

"Listen, I need your number so I won't have to pop up on you like this again." Cole gave Ramir his number. After storing the number, Ramir stepped out of the Audi.

"Hey, quick question," Cole said while also stepping out.

"What up."

"I need to show you something."

"What you got?"

Cole grabbed his briefcase from the back seat and placed it on the trunk of the Audi. He reached in and grabbed the card the Cash told him to take. "What does this represent?" he asked, handing the card to Ramir.

"Yo, what the fuck?" Ramir blurted out, snatching the card from Cole's hand. "Where you get this from?"

"The agents that were at the penitentiary handed that to Cash before they left. It seemed like some sort of threat. What is it?"

Ramir hesitated for a second, not knowing if he could trust Cole. If he told Cole the meaning of the card, there was no telling what Cole would subsequently do with that information. Ramir didn't trust anyone but the Street Kings. Being born and raised in the streets of Bankhead showed him there was no loyalty in the streets. Loyalty only came from fear. In his head, people were only loyal because they feared what would happen to them if they weren't. Cole already knew what Ramir was capable of because five minutes prior, Ramir was ready to put a few hot ones in him. "Let's just say these cards were left on a few dead bodies. I saw something 'bout it on the news a while back."

Cole saw right through Ramir's fabricated answer. Based on his initial reaction and the way Cash panicked, it didn't take a rocket scientist to figure out the Street Kings were behind the cards left on dead bodies. "Listen I don't know why this was given to Cash but since it was, I suggest you figure out a way to clean it up before things get messy."

"How the hell am I gon' do that?"

"If the F.B.I. has these cards and the plan is to take your boys down, then you need to put the cards back on the radar."

"What the fuck is that supposed to mean?"

Cole shook his head. He couldn't believe the words that were about to come out of his mouth. "Make some more cards appear on some more bodies. They can't pin the evidence on men that are locked up."

Ramir lit up when he heard Cole's suggestion. It was music to his ears. Heads were going to roll, but now there would be some strategy behind it. There were already problems in the streets that needed to be dealt with but it seemed like Ramir would be able to kill two birds with one stone. "Who else knows about this?"

"No one. Cash did tell me to get in contact with his girl. I cleared my schedule to meet with her. She should actually be at my office soon."

"Tell her to call 'Ramir' once she leaves your office."

"Is there anything you want me to do about the card?"

"Naw, I'll handle this. You just worry about getting my cousin and his homies out of jail."

"I'm on it. The Feds aren't playing fair, so I need a list of everyone who isn't accounted for from the arrests at the party. There's no telling what city everyone could be at."

"That's everybody. The rest of us got kicked loose the next morning after they tried to get info from us. The only people they kept was Cash, Don, Ace, and Trey."

"Trey?"

"Yeah. He never came back home, so I'm assuming he's locked up somewhere too."

"Well, I never got any paperwork for him regarding this case."

"What the fuck is that supposed to mean."

"It means that he was never charged with a crime. If he was arrested that night and not charged, my only guess is that he is cooperating with the investigation."

"Cooperating? You mean he's snitchin'." Ramir wasn't prepared to receive this type of news. He was filled with rage. "Just make sure you take care of my folks and get them out of those jails. I'll flush out the rat and handle everything else."

# Chapter 7

"Give me one reason why I shouldn't blow your fuckin' head off bitch, and it better be a good fuckin' reason."

The woman kneeling in front of Ramir looked up with pleading eyes. She panted heavily, trying to take a deep breath, but the duct tape wrapped around her mouth and jaw kept her mouth firmly shut. Her broken, bloody nose made it even more difficult to breathe. Her body was limp, and she didn't even attempt to break free. There was duct tape securing her hands behind her back and her feet together. The pain that shot through her body was excruciating. Her head was throbbing, and blood dripped from a large laceration on her forehead.

Ignoring the woman on her knees, Nate paced around the construction site to make sure everything was in order. He peered down into the hole beneath that had been dug out specifically for their guest. A cement truck was backed up to the hole. The mixer drum was spinning and tilted, causing the cement to slowly pour into the hole. He craved for moments like this, although he enjoyed torturing his adversaries more rather than a quick death. Nate was Ramir's best friend but was more ruthless than Ace. He truly enjoyed the art of making families suffer. He earned a reputation as a force to be reckoned with in the streets of Atlanta. Each beef he ever had ended with someone's body missing and never being recovered.

On the other hand, Ramir felt completely different about the moment. Stepping backward, a sense of remorse came over him. All of the memories of him and the woman began to race through his head. Family events, baby showers, college graduations, and many more moments that were memorable to him. He lowered the pistol that he had pointed at the woman and tucked it into his waistband.

"Yo Nate!" Ramir yelled out, before nodding his head toward the bloody woman. Nate pulled out a switchblade and made his way over to her. He grabbed her by the head and began stabbing. After about six jabs, he ripped off the duct tape that he just punctured. His stabs were far from precise, so blood and flesh from her lips were stuck to the tape. The woman began coughing up the large amount of blood that had flowed into her mouth.

Ramir shook his head and paid close attention to the woman cringing on the ground. Death would have probably been a relief to her at that moment. Nate reached down and grabbed the woman by her hair, forcing her to look at the man she had betrayed.

"Ramir, please don't do this," Naomi pleaded. Begging for her life was the last resort, but it was the only chance she had of surviving the encounter. "Ramir please, I didn't say anything to the cops."

"Listen, this is out of my control."

"It's not. They will listen to you. You can stop this."

Ramir reached into his pocket and pulled out his ringing phone. He answered the phone and turned it toward Naomi. She peeked up and saw the face that was on the screen.

"What's going on Naomi? Long time no see."

"Chris, please. I had nothing to do with this," she pleaded before spitting out a glob of blood.

"You had everything to do with this."

She looked at him sitting in his jumpsuit. She didn't even want to know how he was able to get a phone in his cell. "I didn't. I told Trey not to do it. I promise you."

"I need you to tell me exactly what happened and don't lie to me."

"Trey only told me that he got picked up by the Feds. He didn't tell me why. He said he had to leave because he agreed to cooperate with the Feds against y'all. I told him not to. You have done so much for us and our family; I knew nothing good would come from him testifying against everyone. Once Trey was killed, the Feds had me and the kids in a safe house and tried to get me to testify against y'all. I told them I didn't know nothing. I promise you."

"How did Trey die?" Cash asked.

"What do you mean? Y'all shot him when we were in Jamaica."

"Shot him, huh?"

"Yeah. Wait, you didn't know? That wasn't y'all? What the fuck?" Naomi realized Cash wasn't asking about the details because he knew them, he was asking because he wanted to know them.

"Naomi, that wasn't us. I thought Trey was locked up with us."

"He was. I think that was all a part of the Feds plan. They wanted you to think he was charged."

Cash shook his head. Everything Naomi was saying seemed so unbelievable. "Well, we ain't the ones who shot him."

"So then who was it?"

"I have no idea. What made you think it was us?"

"Because I knew what Trey did and he told me about the Jamaicans y'all used to hang with."

"Oh really? He told you about the Jamaicans?"

"Y-Yes," Naomi said reluctantly.

"So tell me something. Trey was the reason Ace's party got raided?"

"Yeah, that was him."

"You were at the party. So, you knew the raid was going to go down, and you didn't say shit?"

"Chris, it's not like that. I didn't know —"

"Don't you dare try and lie to me. You knew it was going down and you didn't say shit, right or wrong?"

"R-Right," Naomi replied. She began crying hysterically. "C-Chris, please. Please let me go. I won't say anything to anyone. I promise you."

"Yo, Nate."

"What's up, boss?'

"Make it slow," Cash ordered before hanging up the phone.

"No. Don't do this," Naomi begged once she saw the sinister grin on Nate's face.

He expected Cash to spare the woman that was once considered his sister. Naomi was a Street Queen. She was hood royalty and was treated as such. Women worshipped the ground she walked on and envied her at the same time. As soon as word got out that Trey was a rat, a price went on her head. She had nowhere else to go when the Feds cut her loose. The moment she stepped foot into the hood, Ramir and Nate snatched her up.

Nate wasted no time, sending a swift punch to Naomi's kidneys. Blood poured from her mouth, as she violently coughed up her lungs.

"Ramir," Naomi murmured.

Ramir looked down at her but didn't say a word. He remembered when he ran errands for Trey and Naomi back when he just joined the crew. Her little brother, Deuce, used to party with Ramir and Nate. He was going to be devastated because Naomi was all he had. She took care of him, and Trey was molding him to become a man and a hustler. Trey wanted Deuce to finally be able to get on his own two feet. They treated him good and kept money in his pockets. They were all once a family.

"My kids. Where are my kids?" She barely got the words out her mouth.

"Your kids? I thought you'd never ask," Nate said as he chuckled at her agony.

He signaled to someone that stood in the shadows. Naomi heard footsteps but didn't have enough energy to get up and see who was approaching. The footsteps got closer and then passed. She could see a large man dragging three duffle bags behind him.

"Nooooooo!!!" Naomi screamed when she saw an arm hanging out one of the duffle bags. "What did you do to my babies?"

"The same thing I'm 'bout to do to you," Nate said before kicking Naomi in the face.

Her body had become numb to the pain, and she was beginning to lose consciousness. Each blow was more brutal than the last. Naomi briefly faded out. One moment she was staring at a black Timberland boot that was striking her in the face and the next she was looking at the stars passing by as someone dragged her across the concrete. One of Naomi's eyes was swollen shut. Her vision was blurred, and she could barely make out the figure that stood before her. She wasn't sure if it was Nate or Ramir. For all she knew, it could have been another one of their goons. Whoever it was cocked their leg back and kicked her right in the gut, which sent her falling into the hole that was being filled with cement.

"Baby I don't think this is a good idea," Naomi said. "We can't do this to the family."

"Family? This ain't no family. I started this shit, and now I'm going to finish it!" Trey barked.

"You and Chris started this."

"Fuck that. He has no vision. He is small time; has been and always will be."

Trey continued packing his bag, while Naomi still tried to process everything he told her. She couldn't even imagine leaving their beautiful mansion to live life in hiding. She had plans to meet up with Don and talk about opening a salon, but Trey was greedy and only wanted to triple the amount of work he distributed.

"So what is your plan?"

"We take all the cash we got, and we leave. Me, you, and the kids. The Feds have agreed not to put restrictions on our passports, so I plan to ditch them when we get overseas. Cash won't be able to touch us, and the Feds can take down this weak ass empire."

"An empire you helped build. Did you forget that?"

"I don't give a fuck. It will burn to the ground."

"Trey, I love you but I want no parts of this."

"Well if you don't come with me, then you can spend the rest of your life in prison like the rest of them because the Feds are going to come knocking, whether they have me or not."

"So you going to snitch on me too?"

"I'm taking down everybody. Pick which side you want to be on when the smoke clears."

"Where would we go?"

"Anywhere. China, Iran, Taiwan, Cuba, you name it. We can go anywhere you want."

"Let's go to Jamaica."

"We can't go there. They have extradition."

"Let's just go for a weekend and then I don't care where else we go."

"I don't think that's a good idea."

"Please. Do it for me and the kids."

"Ok, but just for the weekend. I don't want the Feds or Street Kings finding us."

"When are we going to leave?"

"Right after Ace's party."

Naomi jumped into Trey's arms. She didn't agree with his decision to turn on the organization, but she also didn't want to risk going to jail. Unfortunately, Trey was the love of her life and she was loyal to him. Just being wrapped in his arms made her feel good.

A loud knocking sound made Naomi regain consciousness. The cement slowly filled the hole. Naomi barely snapped out of the daze and laid her eyes on the lifeless body of her oldest son. His body had fallen out of the bag when thrown into the hole. There was nothing she could do for him, as she was still bound by the duct tape and badly bruised. It didn't take long for her son's body to be submerged in the cement. This was it. Her time on earth had come to an end. She had put her children's lives at risk, and now they had been killed. The cement had now reached her mouth, her nose, and then her eyes. A tear ran slowly down her face, and she took her last breath. Nate stood over the site until every drop of the cement mixture covered her head. Their actions were a grim reminder of the mercilessness of the organization. As soon as the hole was filled, he took off with the rest of the group.

# Chapter 8

Ramir looked out the window of the stash house, checking to see if the guests he was waiting for had arrived yet. The corner of Pond Street NW and Andrew J Hairston Boulevard NW was jumping. Home of the Bankhead Boyz gang, there was a lot of activity going on in the neighborhood. The corner boys were out making sales, and the lookout boys were patrolling the block. They had to keep an eye out for cops and anyone that looked suspicious. In that neighborhood, there was no telling what was going through some of the heads of the people that were born and raised there. Every street was riddled with abandoned homes and narcotics. There were times small crews have come through and stuck up some of the corner boys. The stick-ups subsequently resulted in the loss of several young lives. Candlelight vigils surrounded streetlights, wooden boards covered windows that were shattered during drive-by shootings, and RIP graffiti tagged up abandoned cars on the street.

Although Ramir was the distributor for the Bankhead Boyz, he hung around to check on them too. He started out in their position before Ace helped bring him up through the ranks. The crew was loyal to the Street Kings and always has been. The loyalty led to Ramir getting the approval to stick a stash house in the neighborhood. Disguised behind the low-level drug sales, no one knew Ramir moved hundreds of thousands of dollars in product, guns, and cash through the neighborhood monthly. Since getting under the Street Kings, things for the Bankhead Boyz have been fairly peaceful. They hadn't had any major beefs and if they did, Ramir supplied them with enough firepower to eliminate any threat that came their way.

Word traveled fast around Atlanta. When news of the arrests began to spread, it was expected that anyone copping weight of the Street Kings was to remain patient until Ramir was able to restock their inventory. The arrests were an obvious setback, but he was ready to get back to business. Out of every crew in the city, all but a few waited for Ramir to get in contact with them. Those who didn't wait were rumored to have moved on to another connect for their product. Finding another connect was not only a violation of the street code but also disrespectful to the organization. There was only one way Ramir knew how to deal with disrespect, and that was to set an example of those who are disobedient.

After Ramir ran up on Cole, Cash's girl contacted him. They concluded that Ramir's method would be best in this situation, but the job should be contracted out. If the police were already looking into Ace and the Street Kings for their unsolved murder cases, then using people associated with the organization would bring the heat back on them. They needed people that couldn't be traced, and she knew exactly who to contact to get the job done.

When the van pulled up to the corner of the block, the driver beeped the horn five times and then flashed the high beams. One of the lookout boys, riding his bike in the street, saw this and headed up on the grass toward an abandoned home. He ran around back and squeezed through a wooden panel that covered the back door.

"They are here," the boy announced.

"Ok, bring them back here," Ramir responded.

The young boy ran out front and approached the van. After speaking with the driver, the young boy got back on his bike and hit the streets. The driver and other six occupants of the van exited and headed to the back of the house. The wooden panel on the back door was now partially open, and two men stood by the door, armed with shotguns. The occupants from the van were allowed access into the home.

Upon entering the home, they walked into the small kitchen. Ceiling tiles were missing, cabinet doors were hanging off, the flooring was stained, and the refrigerator was missing. A woman was at the stove cooking crack cocaine, and two others were bagging up on the countertop. They were completely naked. Their slim bodies were appealing to the visitors passing through the house. The dining room was in no better condition. Broken wood panels covered the floor and holes decorated the drywall. A small table was centered in the room. A curvy woman sat at the table counting thousands of dollars. She was also naked. Her hair was pulled up into a bun, allowing her gorgeous face to be on display.

The occupants were led straight into the living room area, which was converted into a storage room. Several large safes lined the walls. A large table was cornered in the room, and Ramir was sitting in front of the table.

"Thanks for coming," he said, greeting the occupants of the van.

"No problem. I heard you have a little problem that you need us to take care of," one of the men said with a slight Jamaican accent.

"Yeah. I have four problems that need to be taken care of ASAP. It's up to you guys how you want to handle them."

"So what do you need us to do?"

"We need three of these people wiped off the face of the earth. I have pictures of each of them and also addresses, descriptions of their cars, and their known hangout spots."

"What if they are with people when we catch them?"

"You can take them out too."

The men stepped forward to get a glimpse of their intended targets. There were a total of four piles of paperwork on the table. There were photographs on the top of each pile. The first two piles focused on two different men and detailed information on both of them. The third pile had photos of two men and their information. "So what's going on with these guys?" one of the men asked while pointing to photos in a fourth pile.

"This is a very specific job. We need you to get these three motherfuckers for us, but we want you to bring them to us alive. Getting them isn't going to be easy, so I'll make sure they don't see y'all coming."

One of the men began distributing the piles of paperwork amongst his team. He grabbed the fourth pile and held on to it for himself. "We are going to need some tools to complete these jobs."

Ramir signaled to two goons that were standing in the opposite corner of the room. The men opened two of the safes on the wall and began walking items over to Ramir. Everyone in the room watched as the men carefully placed each item on the table. There were over twenty handguns, rifles, and shotguns spread out across the table. Boxes of ammunition accompanied each firearm. Ramir also threw a red backpack on the table.

"There is information for a hotel in here and ten grand which should cover any expenses you guys have for now. Payment for handling these jobs has already been worked out with your boss. There are also four sets of keys for rental cars that y'all can use. The hotel and the cars are already paid for. We have women that will be stopping by the hotel later tonight, to officially welcome you to Atlanta. I know y'all had a long flight from Jamaica so hopefully, they will keep y'all relaxed. I also stuck some prepaid phones in there just in case y'all have any questions."

"Listen man. This is more than enough. Thank you."

Ramir shook hands with each of the visitors. He made sure his men helped them load the van up with their new toys. He was happy the jobs were going to be handled, but he wasn't used to being hands off when it came to handling important business. Ramir loved putting in work and wanted to take care of these loose ends. A storm of shit was going to come after the Jamaicans handled their business and he knew it was going to hit hard. His next move was preparing all the loyal crews for any retaliation that might take place. Although the idea of using outside hittas was to avoid having anything traced back to the Street Kings, Ramir knew nothing ever goes as planned. He had to have a plan B, and it had to be thorough. The freedom of the Street Kings depended on it.

# Chapter 9

The black Chevy Impala sat in the parking lot at the intersection of Julian Street and Dalvingley Street. The odor of burnt marijuana filled the car as the occupants passed around a fat blunt filled with sativa. All eyes seemed to be focused on The Cut apartments. There was light foot traffic on Dalvingley Street, mostly because three dealers were out front providing the local junkies with their fix. The three were youngsters that were part of the D-Block gang. The gang used to sell for the Street Kings, but since the arrests, the head of the D-Block gang found another coke connect and continued their business. It didn't take long to realize there was no loyalty in the streets. As the occupants in the Chevy continued watching the trio, they noticed the cash was being handed to one person in particular. A heavy-set dealer named Los. Los was half-Black and half Puerto Rican. He stood out on the block because of the tattoo of the Puerto Rican flag on the right side of his neck. He had long braids and a full beard. Los' older brother, Antonio, was the head of the D-Block gang and Los was always on the streets to make sure nobody shorted his brother's income.

For years, Antonio copped his work from Cash and Trey, but with them being behind bars he reached out to a Colombian connect for his re-up. Like many of the local dealers, Antonio was impatient and needed to keep his money flowing. The Colombians prices were higher, but a drought on D-Block would have been damaging to Antonio's business.

"Oh yeah, Tone is going to be happy to know that business is booming as usual," Los said to the other two.

"Yeah, I thought we were going to slow down after Cash and 'em got booked," one of the dealers replied.

"Man, fuck them. We ain't depending on nobody to eat. These are our streets." Los looked up and down the block, with his chest poked out. He was much more hotheaded than his older brother and the one who found the new cocaine connection. Once the Street Kings were locked up, Los called around to find out who had product for sale. He was able to get in touch with three brothers who supplied his gang with multiple keys of coke. Their price was slightly higher than the Street Kings but it didn't matter to Los, as long as he was able to keep D-Block poppin'.

The doors on the Chevy slammed shut, and two men leaned on the running vehicle. They continued watching the dealers while finishing off the blunt. Their bloodshot eyes followed the dealers as they paced back and forth, making sale after sale. About five minutes passed, and the foot traffic began slowing down. All three men stayed outside, but for the most part, they were just conversing. The men from the Chevy began walking towards the entrance of The Cut. Dressed in all black, the two men blended in with the dark scenery. The streetlights had been intentionally broken by the D-Block gang, which made it difficult for police officers to see the drug activity when they rode by while on patrol. It also made it hard for narcotics officers to conduct surveillance in the area without immediately being spotted by the locals. Each of the men walked with a slight limp. They wore knit caps on their heads, and dreadlocks hung down from under the hats. They walked up to the entrance of the apartments and were spotted by Los.

"Who the fuck are y'all?" Los asked while pulling up his shirt and displaying a nine-millimeter handgun that was tucked in the waistband of his sagging jeans. The two other dealers stood behind Los, reaching into their waistbands too. The odds seemed to be favoring them, seeing as though it was three against two.

Although Los was aware of the men's approach, he wasn't ready for their response to his actions. Both men reached down, pulled out pistol-grip shotguns from the leg of their pants, and began blasting at the dealers.

BOOM! BOOM! BOOM! BOOM! BOOM!

Each shot roared like thunder in the quiet night sky. Neighbors that were close by began scattering like roaches, not knowing exactly who the shots were intended to hit. Los couldn't even draw his gun before one of the slugs ripped off a chunk of flesh from his right shoulder. He immediately dropped to the ground, cowering in pain. Blood soaked his shirt as the burning sensation began to worsen. Without the use of his right arm, he attempted to reach for his gun with his left hand. His efforts were unsuccessful because his sagging pants dropped to his ankles when he fell to the ground. He watched as his two cohorts were gunned down next to him. Slugs tore through their chests and legs, leaving them mangled in pools of blood. There was a warm, wet feeling in Los' groin area as the two shooters stood over him.

"Yo, yo, yo, what the fuck y'all want?" Los asked as he scooted away from the men. "Who are y'all?"

Silence filled the air as the shooters slowly walked up on him. The handgun had slid out the waistband, but Los was too focused on his gunshot wounds to even attempt to reach for the gun again. One of the shooters smacked him across the face with the hot barrel of the shotgun, which opened up a fresh gash that began leaking blood. The warm fluid ran down the left side of Los' face as his head began throbbing.

"Come on man, don't do this. I got two stacks on me and some bundles of coke. Y'all can take that shit. Just don't shoot me."

The men continued advancing as Los squirmed backward. He did his best to get away from the reapers that held his fate on the tip of their trigger fingers. Los couldn't stand the pain any longer, so he stopped crawling backward. There wasn't much more he could do to get himself out of the current situation. "What the fuck do y'all want?" Los asked as he cringed in pain. One of the shooters reached into his pocket and pulled out an item. He showed the item to Los before tossing it at the whimpering man.

"Tone!" Los yelled out, hoping someone would run and get his brother. "Tone!"

As soon as Los attempted to yell a third time, one of the shooters shoved the barrel of the shotgun down his throat. The warmth of the barrel was agonizing. It was clear now why the men came after him and his crew. He knew that his day had come to dance with the devil, so he did nothing but shut his eyes, causing a tear to run down his cheek. After the first tear, more began to run his face with the blood.

BOOM!

# Chapter 10

All was quiet on McDaniel Street in the Pittsburgh section of Atlanta. That was until the bass from some car speakers began rocking the neighborhood. A black Range Rover pulled up to the intersection of University Avenue. Music was blaring out the cracked windows and cigar smoke was escaping into the cool night air. The traffic light turned green, but the driver of the Range Rover never accelerated. He rolled his window down and threw the remainder of the cigar out the window. The music he was blasting was now turned down and could barely be heard outside the car.

"Yo, shawty!" he yelled out to a woman that was crossing the street. She ignored him and continued walking on University Avenue. His eyes scanned her body, noticing every curve she had to offer. She was in relaxed attire, wearing a hoodie and a pair of tights. She had the body of an Instagram model, and he wanted her in the worst way.

"What's ya name sweetheart?"

"Reana," she replied as she eyed up his nice ride.

"Well, I'm Mack. Where you 'bout to go?"

"To a friend's house."

"Where ya friend live at?"

"Damn," Reana said, wondering why he was all in her business. "Why you want to know all 'dat?"

"Cuz."

"Cuz what?"

"Cuz you said you're going to a friend house and seeing as though we're friends now, that must mean you're coming to my crib," Mack said jokingly.

Reana burst out in laughter. She tried to compose herself, but that last statement was too outrageous to maintain her composure. "That was so fuckin' corny." It was difficult for her to control her laughter.

"Damn it's like that shawty?" Mack asked with an attitude. He wasn't used to rejection when it came to women. Mack was one of the biggest coke dealers in the Pittsburgh area, and women lined up to get a chance to date him. He had a weakness for a pretty face and round ass. It was no secret that he was generous to his companions. So many women looked at him as a quick come up and he didn't care. He looked at seduction as an art form and spoiled each of his women. So for Reana to reject him was like a smack in the face. It was a first for him.

Reana continued walking. Mack could see that she was still chuckling over the situation as she made her exit. *Fuckin' stuck up ass bitch*, he thought as he sparked up a blunt. He inhaled the soothing herb, allowing the smoke to fill his lungs before blowing it into the air. The Range Rover pulled up slowly next to Reana as her heels clicked on the concrete. Mack pulled up slightly ahead of Reana and exited the Range Rover. She slowed down her stride and looked him up and down. Mack was fresh from head to toe. He was sporting a puffy Moncler coat, Balmain jeans that were sagging off his waist and a pair of Moncler boots. Reana was a fashionista, so she immediately recognized the luxury clothing Mack was draped in.

"You are very persistent."

"I think we got off on the wrong foot."

"You think? I just met you, and you're telling to come to your house," Reana scoffed, pushing her mouth up in disgust.

"I didn't mean to disrespect you. How about we go out and get a bite to eat. Let me show you around my hood." Mack reached into the slim, boot cut jeans and pulled out a wad of cash.

"I can give you the world."

Reana's eyes lit up when she saw the roll of hundred dollar bills in Mack's grip. Her lips went from being pushed up to very wide, as a gorgeous smile spread across her face. "Well what are we waiting for?"

she asked while trotting over to the passenger side of the Range Rover.

*Works every time*, Mack thought. He knew very few women could resist the sight of cash. He hopped in the vehicle and took off. "So where we going?" he asked Reana, biting his lip and basking in his moral victory.

"How about we go check out the Speakeasy Lounge," Reana suggested.

"That spot down off of University Avenue?"

"Yup." Reana placed her hand on Mack's thigh. He looked over at her and smiled, knowing he had other plans rather than heading straight to the lounge.

Mack drove through a maze of streets, which seemed to be a much longer route to the lounge than Reana had expected. Once he began slowing down, Reana looked around and noticed they were in some random neighborhood and nowhere near the lounge. It was expected that Mack would try something slick to get some pussy and Reana intended to play right along and give him what he wanted.

"What are we doing here?" she asked, confused as to why they stopped in a secluded area.

"I want to smoke before we head into the lounge," he replied. Mack took a puff of the blunt and passed it to Reana. She grabbed the blunt with her right hand, while her left hand caressed his thigh. She wrapped her full lips around the blunt and slowly inhaled. Mack became excited, hoping Reana would be wrapping her lips around him next. She blew the smoke out and sank into the passenger seat. Mack couldn't help but admire her beauty. Her smooth brown skin, dark eyes, thick lips left him craving her. Normally he would have made a move by now, but she seemed to be in control.

"You like that?" Mack asked referring to the weed that they were both smoking.

"It's ok," she replied.

"Ok? Shawty this is some of the best weed in the city. It doesn't get much better than this," he barked. One thing Mack was proud of was his product. He was known for his quality and after linking up with a new connect, he wanted to make sure his customers would stay satisfied. Reana's comment hit a nerve, and she could see it all over his face.

"Well this ain't gon' get us high enough, so what else do you have?"

"Well damn, how high you trying to get?"

"I want to have some fun," Reana whispered in his ear as her hand brushed by his groin area. She felt something stiff and smiled.

"Oh, shit, my bad," Mack muttered while adjusting his belt. Before Reana could say a word, he unbuckled his pants and pulled it out.

"Damn!" Reana's response was priceless. She liked what she saw. "Can I touch?"

"Hell yeah, just be careful."

Reana reached down and grabbed Mack's piece. He could tell she was intrigued and turned on. She kept readjusting herself in the seat. "What kind of gun is this?"

"A Springfield XD. It's my favorite piece. We put in a lot of work together."

She gently ran her hand across the handle before gripping the handgun. Mack let her remove it from his waistband as he reached in the backseat for a duffel bag. He felt around the rear floor area and pulled the bag up toward him. Although Reana was playing with his gun, she peeked over and watched him open the bag. Mack stuck his hand inside the bag and began tugging at something. He removed a credit card from his pocket, scooped a pile of white powder from the bag, and placed it on the dashboard. "Now this will get you high."

"What is it?"

"The finest coke in the A, straight from Colombia," Mack said proudly.

He reached in his pocket and pulled out one of the hundred dollar bills from his wad. He rolled it up, placed it in the small white mound, and used his nostril as a vacuum to snort the substance. The powder entered his nostril, and he felt a quick jolt of energy rush through his body. He began sniffing as snot began to run down his nose.

"Now let's have some fun." Mack was leaning over toward Reana and had his hands all over her body. She wasn't comfortable and felt herself losing control. The coke made Mack a tad bit aggressive. "Ohhhh," he yelled out as he felt a hand squeezing his hard dick.

"You gon' let me taste this?" Reana asked as she began stroking him firmly.

"Of course, baby." Mack leaned forward, grabbed the hundred dollar bill, and snorted another hit. This time he licked his lips and leaned back in the seat. He was ready for Reana to put her mouth on him. It was time for him to get what he deserved.

BANG! BANG! BANG! BANG!

Bullets ripped through the front windshield, shattering the glass. Mack's body jerked as the bullets pierced his flesh and entered him. More shots were fired, and the gunmen were sure not let him live to see another day. They continued firing until the slides on their guns locked back. Chunks of plastic from the steering wheel flew through the air, along with glass and blood. Reana had her back pressed against the passenger door, ensuring she was clear from the gunfire. Suddenly the door opened, almost causing her to fall out the Range Rover. She looked back and was face-to-face with a dark-skinned male, who had the look of pure evil in his eyes. A long scar extended from his left eyebrow, down to his wide nose. Reana saw the gun in the man's hand but noticed it was empty. He wasn't prepared to see her raising the Springfield XD, so he stepped back from the vehicle.

BANG!

A single shot through the right side of his head. Blood and brain matter blew out the left side of Mack's head and redecorated the interior of the vehicle. Reana stepped out and slid the gun into her purse. She reached back into the car and went through Mack's pockets, removing the large wad of cash he had flaunted earlier in the night. She then tucked a playing card halfway in the pocket— **THE QUEEN OF HEARTS**. She stuffed the cash into her purse and opened the back door. She grabbed the duffel bag and tossed it to the gunman that was standing behind her. The bullet she sent through the side of Mack's head left chunks of flesh on the bag, but it didn't faze either of them. A black Chevy Impala came whipping around the corner with no lights. It pulled up to the Range Rover, and Reana and the two gunmen approached the Chevy. The gunmen entered the back and quickly shut the door. Reana pulled the band out of her head, allowing her goddess locs to drop from the bun they were held up in and hang down naturally. She looked back at the mutilated Range Rover and then entered the Chevy, which sped off into the night.

# Chapter 11

Willis Jamison was in his late forties and well known throughout Greenville, North Carolina. He had a beautiful wife and three children at home and worked as a marketing consultant. Willis Jamison spent a lot of time in Charlotte and volunteered around Atlanta to speak with the troubled youth. He was a light-skinned and professional looking man. At six foot tall, he weighed approximately two hundred and forty pounds. He had a thick beard, burley stomach, and wide hands. Behind the facade Willis put on display were many dark secrets. One of those secrets was a cocaine addiction that fueled his trips back and forth to Atlanta.

Inside the dark hotel room, Willis was lying flat on his stomach on top of the comforter. A cool breeze was coming through the window and had him feeling great. He slowly emptied a powdery substance on his hand, between his thumb and index finger. Willis placed his hand beneath his nose and sniffed the powder until it filled his nostrils. He leaned back, hitting the back of his head on the headboard, which startled his guest.

Willis sank down into the sheets and rolled over on his side. He pulled his companion close allowing his soft penis to be felt against their buttocks. It was time to expose another one of Willis' dark secrets. His hand caressed the chest of the young, sixteen-year-old boy that was cuddled next to him. Willis was a predator. When he came to Atlanta to speak with the youth, he was scouting out his next victims. He was fond of young boys, and no one had a clue. He knew better than to do his dirt back in North Carolina because he didn't want to risk his wife finding out. She would kill him if she found out, especially since they had two young sons and a daughter together.

Willis kissed the back of the boy's neck and pressed his now erect penis between the boy's cheeks.

"Wait, let me get a drink," the young boy requested.

Willis reached toward the floor and grabbed the bottle of Bankers Club Vodka. He handed the bottle to the boy and watched as the youngin' took several swigs of the strong beverage. Willis knew most of these kids wanted attention, so he lured them with the promise of cash and drugs. He would do with them as he pleased and eventually put them on the block, to sell his coke.

"Here try some of this," Willis suggested as he stuck his hand in front of the boy's face. This wasn't the first time Willis had given the boy coke, and he knew the troubled child wouldn't pass up the opportunity to escape reality.

The boy snorted the drug, and his eyes rolled in the back of his head. He never even noticed Willis had entered him. Willis pinned the boy down and had his way with him for fifteen minutes before ejaculating inside the teen. The boy chuckled because it was like clockwork. Willis could never last long and once he was done, he was sound asleep. It was like the quick and disappointing performance from Willis brought the teen back down from his high. The boy looked at the pile of clothes that was placed alongside the bed. He dug in the pockets and grabbed Willis' wallet. His eyes locked on to a small picture of Willis and the Jamison family, as soon as he opened it. In the back of his mind, the boy wondered if the family knew what type of man Willis really was. He reached in the wallet and grabbed fifty dollars from it. *I need to get a snack from the vending machine*, he thought as he put on his clothes. Even though the boy was noisy when getting dressed, Willis was still in a deep sleep.

The boy exited the room and turned to quietly close the door. As soon as the door shut, he felt a hard object being pressed against the back of his head. He went to turn and heard the sound of a gun cocking. A tear flowed down his eyes, and he began to shake.

"Please don't hurt me. I have fifty dollars in my pocket. You can have it," the boy pleaded.

"Open di fuckin doa batty bwoy," a man in a black hoodie ordered.

The boy swiped the key card and opened the door. As soon as the door unlocked, the man pushed the boy forward and rushed into the hotel room. The boy wanted to call out to Willis but saw him sound asleep on the bed. It would have been useless.

"Please don't hurt —"

The sentence wasn't even completed before the butt of pistol struck the back of the boy's head. His knees buckled, and he fell to the floor. He was out cold. The man stepped over the boy's body and walked towards the bed. Willis was in a deep slumber. His snores sounded like a lion roaring. The man stood at the foot of the bed and scanned the room. He was disgusted when he saw that Willis was naked because he put the pieces together once he saw the drugs and alcohol. It was wake up time.

BANG!

"Aghhhhhhh!" Willis screamed at the top of his lungs.

He felt excruciating pain in his right leg. As soon as he reached down to grab his leg, his hands began sliding on a warm fluid. Blood was gushing out of his thigh, and not much could be done to stop the bleeding. Willis grabbed a pillow and attempted to use it as a shield.

"What the fuck is going on? Who the fuck are you?"

The man didn't say anything. He looked at Willis and then raised his gun, aiming it at his target.

"Yo yo yo, what the fuck. You don't have to do this. Who are you?" The pain from the gunshot was getting worst. It was throbbing and spreading throughout his body. His leg also began feeling numb.

"Mi a messenga."

"A messenger. A messenger for who?"

The gunman smiled and then reached into the pocket on his hoodie. After reaching into the pocket, he pulled out a card and showed it to Willis.

"No, no, no. Let me explain. I had no other choice. I have a family. I have kids. I'm sorry. I will —"

BANG! BANG! BANG!

Three precise shots left three holes in Willis' forehead. His head jerked back, and blood poured from the holes. There was no movement; just a brief silence in the room as the smoke from the barrel cleared. The gunman walked over to Willis' limp body. A sinister grin spread across his face. He watched as his target's soul left its vessel and headed straight to hell. He leaned forward and slid the card in his mouth—**THE ACE OF SPADES**.

# Chapter 12

Cole squeezed his stress ball with all his might. The events that took place in the past few days had him on edge. He was constantly looking over his shoulder, hoping no one ran up on him again. He was waiting for paperwork he requested from the Feds, hoping he could put an end to their illegal antics. There was a ton of work that needed to be done. The Ace of Spades card was stuck in his mind. He didn't know how to take that information about multiple bodies being found with the card placed on them. He didn't want to become the next body that was found. He didn't want to be the next notch on the belt of the Street Kings organization. He feared them and was petrified of losing their case.

He had isolated himself from the rest of his firm for the day. He needed time to focus and regroup. He reached into his drawer and pulled out a flask. A quick swig of the warm liquor relaxed him more than the stress ball. He sat back in his leather chair and looked around his office. The custom wood grain desk, expensive paintings on the walls, and picture windows that provided him with a beautiful view of downtown Atlanta were all a reminder of the rewards he received from the risky business he conducted. Cole occasionally went into a slump where it seemed as if he wished he had chosen a quiet life as a real estate or divorce attorney, but then he snaps out of it when he thinks about the millions of dollars he makes annually.

Cole turned on his Mac computer and was ready to get to work. He took another swig from his flask and pulled out all the notes he created regarding the case. It was time to get down to business. A sudden email notification piqued his interest as it popped up on the screen. Once he saw the word *DISCOVERY* on the subject line, he knew he would be spending the entire day in the office. The Feds finally sent over their evidence and he was going to dive right into it all, once he finished typing up an internal memo requesting the assistance of an available civil attorney assist him in convincing a judge to unfreeze his clients' accounts.

"Hey Heather, can I see you?" Cole asked after tapping the intercom on his office phone.

His assistant came right in his office, holding a notepad. "What can I do for you, Mr. Weaver?"

"I need a couple of things. I need you to contact the federal penitentiaries in New Jersey and figure out what time federal agents came to speak with my client,

Donovan King. I need the same done for my client, Ace Newton, who is in Colorado. I know you're going to hate me for this, but I also need you to reach out to the federal penitentiaries in every state to locate Trey Davis. We haven't had any contact with him since this case started, so who knows where they stuck him."

Heather laughed, knowing how tedious the latter task would be. "No problem, sir. Is there anything else?" she asked.

"Yes, I need a list of the top attorneys in Colorado and Jersey. We will retain one in each state for each of the respective clients."

"No problem, sir. I will get on it right away."

"Thank you, Heather."

Cole looked down at the email notification in the corner of his screen and then back up at Heather, who was halfway out the door. "Oh Heather, one more thing."

"Yes, sir."

"Can you go out and grab me a caramel macchiato and some breakfast? It's going to be a long day."

"I sure can. Is there anything else you need?'

Cole smiled. "No that's it for now. I promise." After Heather walked up, he began typing away at the computer. Cole worked diligently for hours on the memorandum and a complaint against the F.B.I. on behalf of his clients. He ran through breakfast and lunch. It was reaching the end of the workday, so his associates were leaving the building. Cole told Heather she could head home for the day and finish her work later. The entire office had cleared out, and he was ready to dive into the discovery from the Feds. Cole took the last swig of alcohol, emptying the flask.

Cole opened the email containing the discovery. The first document he viewed was the criminal complaint that was filed against Cash. The complaint was more than ten pages and was packed with details and circumstantial evidence. Nothing seemed solid, but the details suggested the Street Kings organization's primary source of income was from drug sales. He continued flipping through the document and noticed the F.B.I. had a confidential informant listed as the source of their evidence. Cole began checking the other documents, seeing a criminal complaint for Ace and Don. An arrest record list from the night they were all booked was also included. It shows who was released and who was charged. The Feds only went after the top of the organization. They got the big fish and let all the little fish go. There was also a list of local gangs in Atlanta that the Feds believed the Street Kings were distributing to. There was a ton of effort put into building the case, but Cole didn't see anything that was overly concerning. They were throwing shit against the wall to see what was going to stick. Cole continued scanning the documents but noticed there was no information on Trey. He wasn't listed on the list of individuals arrested, and there was no criminal complaint filed against him. It was as if he didn't even exist in the case. Cole began printing out each document so that he could pick it apart.

The door to the office opened, startling Cole who wasn't expecting anyone to be in the building. "What are you doing in here?" he asked.

"Did you forget that tonight is the networking event over at Polaris? I came to see if you were ready to head over," Heather mentioned. She had gone home and changed into a tight blue dress. She transformed from an assistant into a model, as she strutted toward Cole in her six-inch heels. Her brunette hair was wavy and styled in a manner in which it draped over her right shoulder. She belonged on a runway.

"I totally forgot about that event. I don't think I'm going."

"Come on boss. You can't just work all night long. You know what they say about all work and no play," she said, sitting on the edge of his desk and crossing her legs. The split in the dress revealed her thigh.

"Listen, I hear you but I have a lot of work to get done. Did you make any progress with the penitentiaries?"

"Yeah I did," she responded. Heather dug into her purse, pulled out her Yves Saint Laurent Liquid Matte stain, and began applying it to her lips.

"Well..." Cole asked, wondering why she didn't give him an update.

Heather leaned in toward Cole. Despite the air conditioner pumping in the room, he felt a warm sensation in his chest. Between the liquor and her aggressive approach, things began to heat up. He watched as she got closer toward his face. He stared at her thin lips, wanted to kiss them. "I'll give you what you want if you give me what I want," she whispered in his ear. Her lips brushed against his earlobe with each word.

Cole loosened his tie to avoid becoming a sweaty mess. Heather uncrossed her legs, exposing herself to her boss. Heather reached into her purse again, this time pulling out a small bottle of Crown Royal Apple. Cole's mouth began to water as he craved the dark liquor. After being his assistant for two years, it didn't take long for her to realize he had a weakness for liquor. He would send her on missions to get him bottles at a time, consuming them after busy workdays. Cole was poor at dealing with stress and alcohol was his escape from reality.

Heather opened the bottle and poured a small amount into the bottle cap. She tilted the cap over her leg, allowing the liquor to run down her thigh. Cole pounced right on her. He used his warm tongue to catch each drop that was on her flesh. Heather squirmed as the pleasurable sensation traveled up her leg and into her sweet spot. He grabbed the bottle and chugged a quarter of the contents down. Cole unzipped his pants, sending a chill up Heather's neck. She was ready for it. He hiked his boxers down and revealed his cock. Heather wrapped her hand around the shaft and began jerking him off.

Cole ran his hands up her legs until they were completely under her dress. His hands continued exploring her body until they brushed over her pussy. Realizing she wasn't wearing any panties, Cole dipped his index finger inside of her. Heather moaned and pushed her hips toward him, allowing the finger to travel deeper inside of her. Suddenly a second finger slid in, and he began working her. With one hand grasping on to his tie and the other grabbing the desk, she continued rotating her hips. Cole grabbed her by the waist and pulled her closer to him. His cock was inches away from entering. Heather pulled him in by his tie. The simultaneous actions of their lips touching and him sliding inside of her sent them both in a frenzy. The forty-year-old was no match for his twenty-four-year-old assistant. Her energy and aggression prevented him from gaining any type of control. She was thrusting her hips forward and using her legs to lock him in. Cole's short pumps were a start, but Heather wanted more, a lot more.

"Oh yeah baby, fuck me," she moaned as his hands palmed her ass.

Cole barely lasted five minutes before ejaculating inside of Heather. She couldn't believe that happened. During the few times she imagined fucking her boss, she never expected it to go this way. She was so disappointed, and her grim facial expression showed it.

Cole was embarrassed to say anything to Heather. He pulled up his boxers and zipped up his pants. Heather got up and headed toward the door. "Wait, where are you going?" he asked.

"I'm going to head to the bathroom, and then I'm going to Polaris."

"'But what about the stuff I asked you to handled earlier?"

"Everything I found out is on my desk. You can see what I have so far, and if anything else needs to be done, I will handle it tomorrow," she replied. Heather was pissed about Cole's sexual performance, but she also didn't want to jeopardize her job by being rude to her boss.

Heather headed out, and Cole gathered the paperwork from her desk. He was a bit buzzed, but he was still determined to conquer the night. Sheets were torn from a yellow pad and scribbled on. One sheet was the list of attorneys in Jersey and Colorado. Cole was ready to dig through the list and get some more bodies on the case. He grabbed a couple of other sheets that had been written on by his assistant. She had all fifty states listed and the responses she got when speaking with personnel at each federal penitentiary. Cole carefully reviewed the list. He checked for Trey's name. NEGATIVE. There was no penitentiary with a prisoner with that name. Not being on this list only meant one thing. Trey didn't get charged, or he already flipped. Cole needed to contact Cash with this information.

# Chapter 13

"I'm not dealing with this technical bullshit. I have a fuckin' body over there, and the only witness is that teenager. I don't care if his parents aren't here, he's a fuckin' runaway!" Detective Ali barked.

"He's also a possible suspect in this crime, so we have to follow the law. You know that we can't just go and interrogate juveniles without a parent or guardian present. Just in case you didn't know, the Homicide Unit has the lead on this one anyway. Do you want to lose their investigation before it even begins?" Detective Knowles knew his partner all too well. Detective Ayanna Ali was a ball of fire and took cases personally. If it were up to her, she would have the witness strung up by his feet until she got a confession. She earned her spot as being one of the most productive detectives in the Atlanta Police Major Crimes Unit.

"Why do you think we are here, Cliff? Homicide called us because they know the Street Kings did this."

"We don't know anything yet. All of them are in federal prison, so how are we even going to begin to link this to them, Ayanna?"

"Are you serious? The Ace of Spades card is in his mouth. That's their trademark," Detective Ali scowled. Frustration projected her voice, catching the attention of the other detectives in the room. She hated taking a back seat in investigations but had no choice in this case. She walked toward the window and looked down at the ambulance and sea of police vehicles that filled the street. The rear doors of the ambulance were wide open and the young boy was sitting on the back bumper, wrapped in a blanket. Homicide detectives guarded him, but Detective Ali would rather them ask the boy questions about the events that took place. She wanted answers.

"Is everything alright over here?" Sergeant Joseph Packard asked, noticing the animosity in the room.

He was the on-duty supervisor for the homicide unit and was a no-nonsense type of person. The mean expression on his face let the detectives know that he had come over to set them straight. That night would not be their first run-in with him. Detective Ali and Sergeant Packard had bumped heads during another investigation years ago when they were investigating a murder that was possibly linked to Corey King.

Bearing the nickname "The King of Clubs," he built an empire from drug money and bought up a ton of nightclubs in Atlanta, Miami, and Philadelphia. He was untouchable, seeing as though he surrounded himself with men and women that went to great lengths to protect him. This included local politicians, business owners, and even police officers. One of those officers was a seasoned homicide detective that investigated his murder. He and this detective had a close relationship that dated back to the 1960s when they grew up as kids in the same neighborhood. They were close back then, but as years passed, life took them both on two separate journeys. They both had families but lived two completely different lives on opposite sides of the law. Their lives came together when the detective's son was murdered during an armed robbery in downtown Atlanta.

The detective canvassed the streets for his son's killer and while doing so, learned that his old friend was now one of the biggest drug dealers in that area. Nothing happened in the streets without Corey King knowing about it or having some involvement. When the two men finally crossed paths, the detective asked his old friend for a favor and in twenty-four hours, the streets had the killer dropped off at the detectives' doorstep. The nineteen-year-old shooter was wrapped in a bow for the detective, literally.

After the delivery was made, the detective was indebted to Corey King and his organization. He made sure he protected the drug dealer even though he was never asked. When the Narcotics Unit was onto Corey's trail, the leads would surprisingly disappear. Witness names were delivered to members of his crew unexpectedly, and they were sure to visit each person that considered testifying against the group. A message was sent to the streets and playing cards were left at the scenes of homicides. The cards were always somewhere on the deceased body, but sometimes they were stuffed in the mouths of informants. A style of killing the mob had introduced in the past. It was always the same card—**THE KING OF CLUBS**.

Corey King ruled with an iron fist but as the story goes with any king, there is always someone that tries to take his throne. Everything was going smoothly until federal agents came through Atlanta and launched an investigation against Corey. They received an anonymous tip from a "reliable source" about Corey's drug shipments, meetings, transactions, and connections to many homicides in Atlanta and surrounding areas. Once the Feds were involved, there wasn't much the detective could do to protect his old friend. He no longer had access to case files and witness information. Corey King was on his own, and he knew it. That was up until the homicide unit got a call about a triple homicide and arson in Bankhead. A rookie officer responded to the scene of a car fire in which she discovered there were multiple occupants in the vehicle. The violent flames destroyed any piece of evidence that would have been left for investigators. The bodies in the vehicle were unidentifiable. Everything was destroyed. Everything except a card that was left at the scene. A trail of blood led from the vehicle to a wooden bench and on that bench was a bloody playing card. **THE KING OF CLUBS**. After that night, no one ever heard from Corey King again.

"Everything is fine Sergeant," Detective Knowles answered. He knew that this was a battle that wouldn't be won.

Sergeant Packard glared directly past Detective Knowles and stared a hole into the face of Detective Ali. He despised her. In his opinion, she was a loose cannon and he was sure to put her in her place. The large man pushed his two hundred and sixty-pound frame by her partner and stood directly in front of her, staring into her face. His large stomach just an inch from her petite body, to the point she could smell his sweaty armpits and the faint odor of beer coming from his mouth with the heavy breaths he took.

"Is there a problem?" he asked.

She immediately turned her nose up. "No sir, there is no problem at all. As a matter of fact, we were just leaving."

"I think that's a wonderful idea. I don't think you will be needed in this investigation. We got this."

"I bet y'all do," she mumbled under her breath.

Detective Ali was intelligent. She knew which battles were worth fighting and this wasn't one of them.

There was too much history involved and judging by the crime scene, history would surely repeat itself. The hotel room door slammed as she made a hasty exit. Her partner didn't even follow behind to check on her. Instead, he stayed to smooth things out with Sergeant Packard and to continue gathering details of the case. A cold gust of wind forced her to bundle up her coat as she walked by the parade of police cars. Her boots pounded the rough pavement, as she made her way to her vehicle. The streetlights were shining bright, and tree branches swayed with each frosty gust. *One day he is going to get what he deserves*, she thought while entering her Ford Taurus.

The wind was beating on the windows, and the Ford felt as if it were rocking side to side. Detective Ali's eyes were glued to the hotel. She wanted to go back inside. This case was the first break they had in a while for the investigation she started on the Street Kings. Although federal authorities took over the cases involving the criminal enterprise, several unsolved murders in the city still had to be investigated. There were still drugs being sold on the streets despite the arrests of the men who the Major Crimes Unit believed were the distributors. How was this possible? Did the Feds have the right guys? Had someone else stepped up and taken over in their place? There were so many questions and very few answers.

*Where the fuck is he at?* Detective Ali quickly exited the Ford and looked down the street. The rear doors of the ambulance were wide open, but it didn't seem like the homicide detectives were still focused on hovering around the emergency vehicle. Each step she took was swift, and she was able to slip into the side of the ambulance just as the paramedics were closing the rear doors.

"Can I help you?" one of the paramedics asked after seeing the unknown woman standing in their way.

"Atlanta PD," she said, flashing her badge to them. "I just want to give the boy my card."

The boy was wrapped in a blanket and hesitantly looked back at the detective. Several detectives from the homicide unit had hounded him. They mostly believed the boy was the shooter or somehow connected. He was still in shock from the shooting, and the images of Willis' dead body wouldn't escape his mind. "I'm here to help," Detective Ali whispered as she extended her arm to hand the boy her business card. Despite the honesty and innocence, he saw in her eyes, he couldn't help but focus on the badge that dangled from her neck. *They are all the same*, he thought. The boy turned his head and stayed wrapped up in the blanket.

The ambulance door flung open. "Hey, what are you doing in here?" one of the homicide detectives asked.

"I was just checking on the witness," Detective Ali claimed.

"Witness? Are you referring to our suspect?"

The boy's eyes widened and he sat up on the gurney. "Suspect? I told you I didn't do anything." The boy looked back at Detective Ali. Tears fell from his eyes and his lip quivered. "I didn't do this ma'am. I promise you I didn't."

"I know you didn't," she replied.

"GET OUT THE FUCKIN' AMBULANCE. THIS IS OUR INVESTIGATION, NOT YOURS!" Sergeant Packard ordered as he walked up.

Detective Ali stepped out the ambulance and walked back to her car without saying a word to the men that confronted her. She accomplished what she went in the ambulance to do. With no assistance from the homicide unit, she would have to go back to the drawing board and figure out what her next move would be.

# Chapter 14

"Seeing as though you're smiling, you must have some good news for me," Cash muttered while adjusting his tie. Although it was only going to be for a brief period, it felt good getting out of the prison jumpsuit. The courthouse guards checked Cole Weaver's briefcase thoroughly before allowing him into the meeting room.

"I have great news for you Chris, but I don't want to be the one to tell it to you," Cole said proudly.

"Well, who is going to tell me?"

"You'll see as soon as you finish getting dressed."

Despite the words that came out his attorney's mouth, Cash wasn't too optimistic about the outcome of this court hearing. The prosecutors were out for blood, and Cash was like a rare steak with all the fixings. Ever since they raided his mansion, they have been licking their chops to put him behind bars. They finally got their chance when Trey decided to turn on the crew for immunity on a drug trafficking charge.

Cole walked side by side with Cash, as the guards escorted him into the courtroom. Cash scanned the courtroom, recognizing a ton of familiar faces. There were family members in the front row, followed up by friends and associates of the crew and members of the media. He also spotted Trey's mother and aunt in the crowd as well. They both wore sunglasses but the mascara running down their cheeks was an obvious sign that they were in pain. These two women were like mother figures to Cash and the other members of the crew. Memories of staying at their house for months after his father died were stuck in his head. They were not to blame for Trey's choices, and they will be treated no different than they were prior.

Cole and Cash reached the table where two other attorneys from Cole's firms along with Ace and Don greeted them. Dominic Ricci sat behind Don, and an attorney from Colorado sat behind Ace. The crew had a dream team of attorneys representing them. The heads of the Street Kings greeted each other with handshake hugs. The greetings were reassurance that they were tighter than they had ever been, despite being thousands of miles away from each other. Across from their table were the prosecutor and Federal Agents Miles and Carson. If looks could kill, the Street Kings would be six feet under based on the mean mugging they were doing back and forth with the agents.

"All rise. Federal Court is now in session," the bailiff announced. "Judge Theodore Goldstein presiding. Please be seated."

Judge Goldstein emerged from a back room and took his place on the bench. The older white male was a seasoned judge that ruled his courtroom with an iron fist. There was no room for error in his courtroom because his decisions were made solely off the evidence he was presented with, by both sides. Based on the evidence presented, this could either be an asset to The Street Kings or detrimental. "Good morning, ladies, and gentleman. Calling the case of the United States versus King, Newton, and King. Are both sides ready to proceed?"

"I am ready on the side of the government, Your Honor," the prosecuting attorney stated.

"We are ready for the defense, Your Honor," Cole said.

"Well, the prosecution may begin with opening statements."

The prosecuting attorney stood from his seat and organized the five accordion folders that were spread across the table. He removed a blue folder from the first stack and stood in the aisle. "Your Honor, over the years these three defendants have been the heads of one of Atlanta's most ruthless criminal organizations. Each of them has been charged with multiple counts of drug trafficking, money laundering, conspiracy to commit murder, extortion, and several other related charges. There have been several witnesses that agreed to testify against the defendants, and there is evidence to support that testimony. The evidence I present will prove to you that the defendants are guilty of all the crimes they are charged with." After making his opening statement, the prosecuting attorney sat down next to the agents, confident about the case.

Cole chuckled before rising to his feet. "Good morning Your Honor, I am Cole Weaver and I am here with two other members from my firm and we represent the defendants in this case. As you know Your Honor, under the law each of my clients is presumed innocent until proven guilty. The prosecution has done its best to treat these young men as if they were guilty from day one. They have been incarcerated with no chance at bail for crimes they have not committed. They are entrepreneurs and successful business executives that take care of their families and communities; most of whom are seated in the courtroom today. The federal government has frozen their assets and crumbled each of the businesses they own. Their constitutional rights have been violated in many ways. If you grant a hearing today, you will hear no real evidence against any of my clients and their rights will continue to be violated."

"If I grant a hearing?" Judge Goldstein asked, confused by the statement.

"Yes, Your Honor."

"Tell me why the court wouldn't proceed with a hearing."

"I'm glad you asked that, Your Honor. Despite the lie the prosecutor just told about having multiple witnesses, he only had one. This witness' name was Trey Davis who was arrested traveling from one state to another while in possession of a large amount of drugs. Mr. Davis was found murdered in a hotel in Jamaica, and I'm sure he isn't coming back from the dead to testify." The prosecutor and agents shot each other looks, wondering how Cole obtained that information.

"Is this true?" Judge Goldstein asked the prosecutor.

"Umm, yes it is Your Honor. I have Agent Miles and Agent Carson with me on behalf of the Federal Bureau of Investigation. After speaking with Agent Miles, we believe the defendants had the witness murdered because they knew of his involvement in this case."

"What makes you believe this?" Judge Goldstein asked.

"There was a signature mark left at the crime scene that was specifically used in several unsolved murders in the nineties."

"The nineties? These young men would have been children at that time. What connection is there with them?"

"The suspect in these murders is the father of one of the defendant's —"

"— Who has been deceased for years," Cole chimed in. "This is such a reach, Your Honor, and my defendants have suffered enough. They were all incarcerated when the prosecutor's witness was murdered. They had nothing to do with the murder and had no idea about it until I informed them."

Judge Goldstein removed his glasses and sat forward in his chair. "Is this true? Are you chasing a ghost?"

The prosecutor did not have an immediate answer for the judge. He was desperate and running out of options. "Your Honor, Mr. Davis wasn't our only witness. Mr. Davis' wife, who is also the mother of his children, was present during most of the drug transactions and was willing to testify to what she remembers about each member's involvement in the organization. Although the murder of her husband terrified her, Mrs. Naomi Ikawa-Davis was more than willing to cooperate with this case." Agent Carson gave his partner the side-eye, realizing he never told the prosecutor that Naomi was no longer cooperating with them. After the big blow up at the safe house, she has been in the wind, and there hasn't been any contact with her at all.

"Well, call your witness to the stand."

The prosecutor turned around and looked toward the crowd, searching for Naomi. "The People call

Naomi Ikawa-Davis," he announced. Heads began to turn which was followed up by whispering once everyone noticed that no one was approaching the stand. The bailiff worked his way up the aisle and toward the crowd. There was a brief moment of awkwardness as the prosecuting attorney looked around for Naomi and then caught a glance of the irritated expression on the judge's face. "Where the hell is the witness?" he asked Agent Miles, hoping the judge didn't notice their unpreparedness.

"I have no idea. You know how these scumbags are. They probably had her killed too," Agent Miles suggested.

"Do The People have a witness to call to the stand?" Judge Goldstein asked.

"Umm, Your Honor it doesn't seem like she is here."

"What do you mean she's not here? Where is she?"

"Well Your Honor, it is a possibility that the defendants may have something to do with her absence. Could we request a continuous to ensure her safety?"

Deuce jumped up out of his chair and stormed out the courtroom. The details of the case got the best of him. He suspected the Street Kings had something to do with his sister's disappearance, but after hearing that Trey was snitchin' on his team, Deuce knew he would never see her again.

"Come on, this is absurd," Cole blurted out. "I cannot sit here and allow the prosecution to make up fairy tales about these young men. Your Honor, they have no evidence against my clients and no witnesses to testify. They kept them caged up like animals for nothing. When they raided Mr. King's home, they found no drugs. These men have not been able to provide for their families because of the FBI's wild goose chase, and I beg that you dismiss this case and not grant them a continuance. A continuance will not change the fact that they have no evidence."

Judge Goldstein sat back in his chair and looked at both men. Each of their statements replayed in his head. He began rocking back and forth in the chair as he looked toward the crowd. Children were staring, women crying, and men consoling those in need of comfort. Lastly, his eyes focused on Cash, Ace, and Don. Each of them was dressed to impress, and that is exactly what they did. Nothing about them men seemed as if they were thugs or gangsters. They were dressed in tailored suits and were neatly groomed. The judge also couldn't believe the federal government would pursue these men without solid evidence. There had to be something in those files that could persuade him in some way. His gavel slammed down, grabbing everyone's attention.

"I have made a decision," he said, pausing for a moment. "We have all come here today to hear a case against Christopher King, Ace Newton, and Donovan

King. We have heard the statements made by both sides. The prosecution is responsible for the burden of proof in the case, and they failed to provide a witness for testimony to support the accusations made against the defendants. Based on what we have heard today and the circumstances surrounding this case, I have concluded that the prosecution does not have a valid case against these young men. With that being said, it is my decision to dismiss all charges against the defendants and I want them released from custody as soon as possible."

The courtroom erupted in cheers after the judge made his decision. Don dropped to his knees, thanking God for sparing his life. Ace turned to the crowd with his arms raised, igniting the emotions that everyone was feeling. Cash stayed in his seat and just dropped his head low. He was in disbelief. Hearing the prosecutor pinning the death of Trey and disappearance of Naomi on them was too close to comfort. He wanted more details on Trey's murder. He needed more details. What was the connection the prosecutor was referring to? What unsolved murders was his father involved in? What was the FBI's next move going to be? He had so many questions and not enough answers. He had no idea where to start. Unfortunately, he couldn't celebrate a victory when there was still the possibility of being charged with the Trey's murder.

While everyone in the courtroom was reacting to the judge's decision, Cash kept a stern look on his face. The cheering, sobs, and banging of the gavel were all zoned out. With his heartbeat slowing down, Cash took a deep breath and scanned the room. To him, the victory was just a small one because Trey wasn't the only snake that threatened his empire. There was a laundry list of people waiting to take his spot and run the streets. "The judge just dismissed all charges so tell me why you aren't celebrating," Cole whispered after seeing the expression on Cash's face.

"Cuz we still have other problems to deal with. Those local charges need to be dealt with too because I need to get out that fuckin' cage for good. I can't' go back."

"Are you talking about those murder charges that Atlanta Police was going to stick on y'all?"

"Yeah."

"Well it seems that problem has already been handled on your end," he said, patting Cash on the shoulder.

Cash looked over at Ace, who gave him a head nod. The two men didn't have to speak actual words for them to know that their problem was solved— FOR NOW.

# Chapter 15

The king of the streets was back. Cash stepped out from behind the prison walls and was glad to see Reana waiting for him in the parking lot. She was laced in a deep V-neck, Valentino bodysuit, and matching leather jacket. Sitting on top of a cherry red Mercedes S-Class Cabriolet, Reana thumbed through her phone and waited for her man to emerge. As soon as she laid her eyes on him, she ran toward him and jumped into his arms. It had been months since the couple had been in each other's presence. Cash missed his queen and the way they were lip locking, she knew it.

"I want to thank you for everything you have done for me baby," he said.

"Yuh kno mi wud duh nuhting fi yuh dis did light wuk."

Words couldn't describe the gratitude he felt. If it weren't for Reana, he would still be rotting in a cell. For years, he and his crew ruled the streets of Atlanta and there was no way that anyone that decided to snitch on them would have the opportunity to step into the courtroom. Without witnesses, the prosecutors had no case. Once the news about Trey Davis' death made it to the Feds, they lost the only witness they had that was going to testify and break down every small detail about the Street Kings' operation. The prosecutors wasted so much money trying to keep him in witness protection, but Trey always thought he knew best. Going to Jamaica was Naomi's idea. Trey's arrogance always clouded his judgment and the fact that he felt the need to take a vacation when he knew he was snitching on his own crew is exactly why he met his demise. The same way the Feds caught him is the same way his killer caught him. With all the multiple forms of identification he had, he would have easily been able to lay low in another country, but he just had to bring his kids and Naomi along for the trip. Everyone knew who she was and the Feds didn't arrange to protect her identity, so the killer was able to track their moves through her.

Naomi was around the crew a few times when she started dating Trey. She knew a lot about their operations and could have easily served as a witness in the case against the Street Kings, but she and the kids hadn't been seen since they were removed from the witness protection program. Along with the drug operations, she knew how callous the crew was and what they would do to her and her children if she even considered testifying against them. Due to her lack of cooperation in the case and her unknown whereabouts, the courts had no other choice but to release the Street Kings. Her family was on a search for answers. They wanted to know where she was and Deuce wouldn't stop until he found her.

"Has everyone been taken care of?" Cash asked.

"Everyone except di ones dat start all of dis," Reana replied, knowing there was unfinished business that Cash wanted to handle personally.

He placed his property bag on the trunk of the Mercedes and began digging through it. The bag contained a belt, shoelaces, several keys, jewelry, and his cell phone. Being out of that jumpsuit and back into his designer attire made Cash feel like himself again. As soon as the diamond-encrusted Cuban links dressed his neck, he smiled at Reana.

"Let's get the fuck out of here. I don't ever want to see this place again."

Although he only spent a little over six months in prison, it was more than enough time to make him appreciate the benefits that came with freedom. The fresh air filled his lungs after taking a deep breath. They both got into the car, and Reana wasted no time shoving her hand down Cash's pants. She had a grip on his thick package and was ready to taste him. After being caged like an animal, Cash quickly rose to the occasion. He spent many nights dreaming about the day that he would be able to feel her touch. He leaned over and kissed her. Their tongues intertwined and lips locked, displaying the love they both longed for. The windows began fogging up, and the two began ripping each other's clothes off. Cash was exposed, and Reana was ready to devour him.

"I've been waiting for this," he muttered.

"Mi too baby."

KNOCK. KNOCK.

"What the fuck?" Cash barked, wondering about the banging on his driver's side window.

KNOCK. KNOCK. KNOCK.

The window partially rolled down, and two correctional officers stood next to the Mercedes. One of them was hefty, and the other was thin and old. The hefty officer was wielding an expandable baton, which he pointed in Cash's face. "Does this look like the parking lot of a motel?"

"Naw. We were just leaving."

"You better be," the officer replied, shooting an intimidating glare at the couple.

Cash slammed on the accelerator, leaving the correctional officers standing in a cloud of dust and dirt. He wanted to get back to his life. He wanted to get back to his luxury mansion, steak dinners, and foreign cars. Most of all, he wanted to spend some quality time with the love of his life. As soon as he hit the highway, Reana continued where she left off. She shoved him inside her mouth and salivated until his shaft was soaked. Working her hands up and down his shaft as she sucked the tip caused him to swerve in and out his lane. The sounds of car horns blaring proved that other drivers noticed Cash's erratic driving. He tried his best to drive normally but it was impossible because he knew what was about to come. Reana rotated her head in a circular motion and felt Cash throbbing. It wasn't long before she felt his cream fill her mouth. Cash's head went back, and he let out a loud groan as cum continued pumping out his dick. He was backed up for months and was finally able to release himself. Another horn blared, and Cash noticed he was stopped in the middle of the street at a green light. He continued down the street and looked over at Reana.

"Welcome home baby."

# Chapter 16

Cash pulled up to a warehouse on Murphy Avenue SW, one of the properties the Feds attempted to seize during the case. He entered the warehouse and was immediately smacked in the face by an odor of raw flesh and the stench of feces. He saw Ace and a few of their goons standing in a semicircle. As he approached, the circle opened up and he had a clear view of the Muñoz brothers: Sebastián, Alejandro, and Diego. They were the organization's original drug connects. Their father, Nicolás Muñoz, was the supplier and made sure that any cocaine that came through the streets of Atlanta went through his sons. Doing this ensured that his sons remained rich and the streets depended on them. When Cash and the Street Kings took over, they made a deal with Nicolás to go through his sons, but there was an agreement that the Muñoz brothers would only distribute to them in Atlanta because of the quantity they would purchase at one time. Needless to say, this was an agreement that wasn't adhered to. Once the Street Kings got the product, they would distribute it to the local dealers, which kept everyone in line. There was supposed to be loyalty in the streets, but as soon as things got rough, the snakes began to show. The Muñoz brothers were also distributing to dealers in the Carolinas, Tennessee, and several other states, so they had steady money rolling in. When the Street Kings were arrested, the Muñoz brothers were supposed to wait until they were contacted by Ace's little cousin, Ramir, who was going to take over the distribution on behalf of the Street Kings.

Ramir set up a meeting with the Muñoz brothers, but they refused to give him the shipment. They offered him the coke at retail rather than wholesale. This was their chance to take over Atlanta and distribute directly to the dealers rather than going through the Street Kings. They saw how much money Cash and his crew were bringing in. The lavish lifestyles they were living made the Muñoz brothers envious. Before the recent federal case, they operated without being on the radar of the police when it came to drugs. Most of their heat came from the violence and terror they caused on the street. That was up until they were able to infiltrate the group and find someone that was just as greedy as they were. Although Cash was the face of the organization,

Trey always seemed to be the one to find the drug connects. He started out with marijuana and then somehow got caught up with Maria Muñoz, who was the daughter of Nicolás. She was the daughter of a kingpin and she loved to party. She hooked up with Trey while he was conducting business in North Carolina and after months of dating, she ended up telling him all about her family. Maria is the reason her father was able to take over the A, which was an open market at the time. Trey took this information back to Cash, and they set up a meeting and officially became coke dealers. Although he was in a very good position within the organization, Trey always felt he deserved more credit in the group. He wanted to be second in command but felt like he always came after Ace and Don. He wanted to expand and take over more states, but Cash was content on just having his reach in Atlanta. Since the organization didn't want to expand Trey decided to take his talents to North Carolina and hooked up with Maria. Unfortunately, he was sloppy and scheduled a transaction with a local dealer that happened to be a DEA agent. Once the Feds picked up Trey, it wasn't long before the rest of the Street Kings were behind bars. Once they all were out the way, the Muñoz brothers picked up where they left off.

Cash had zero tolerance for disloyalty. He paced back and forth trying to decide what to do with the three brothers. "Cuando corte la hierba, las serpientes se mostrarán," Cash muttered to himself as he pulled a chair up and sat directly in front of the bloody men. He learned the quote from their father. They were soaking wet; drenched in some type of fluid. They had swelling and lacerations all over their faces. Someone had put a serious beating on the trio. "Cuando corte la hierba, las serpientes se mostrarán. When you cut the grass, the snakes will show. Your father is the one who told me that." There was no response from the brothers; their mouths were gagged. "If you could, I know what you would say. You would say your father is one of the most powerful men in the world and he will have every one of us killed for this type of betrayal," Cash said while chuckling. "Well guess what, he won't find out it was us because he won't find your bodies. We had an agreement and you three motherfuckers betrayed me. Now you will have to suffer the consequences."

No sooner did Cash finish his sentence, Ace stepped forward and flicked the cigar he was smoking at one of the brothers. The liquid they were drenched in quickly ignited, and all three of them caught on fire. Cash looked on as the heat from the flames caused sweat beads to form on his forehead. The screams from the three men were excruciating, but music to his ears. He only wished he could have made it a public display to send a message to anyone else that felt the need to move in on his territory. In the back of his mind, Cash knew that a murder of this magnitude would have started a war with Nicolás Muñoz and his Colombian Cartel. That would have been a war that the Street

Kings wouldn't be ready for. Ace and a few other goons put in work, but not the scale of trying to take out a kingpin. Even with the Dread Headz on call, it still wasn't worth the risk. He watched as skin began to melt from their bones and their faces became unrecognizable. Even the smell of their burning bodies would have turned the average person's stomach in knots.

"Make sure we get rid of these bodies," Cash ordered before walking out of the factory.

∞ ∞ ∞

Cash entered his silver Aston Martin Vantage, and his iPhone began ringing. As soon as he saw the name being displayed on the screen, he immediately looked over at Reana. She leaned over, looked at the screen, and smiled when she saw the name. Cash tapped the screen to accept the call.

"Hola Nicolás."

"Cristóbal, it's good to hear your voice. I was worried when I heard about the unfortunate events that took place," Nicolás Muñoz said, expressing his concern with the arrests.

"Yeah, that was a minor setback. Hopefully, we will be able to move forward with business as soon as things die down and the Feds stop watching my team."

"Yes, we definitely will. Sorry to get straight to the point, but the reason I called is that I haven't heard from my boys in a few days. I know you just got out, but have you heard from them?"

"No Nicolás, I haven't heard from them. I didn't want to reach out this early because I know the Feds are still watching me. Is everything ok? Do you think something happened to them?"

"I sure hope not, but this is odd. Alejandro always checked in with me on a daily basis, so I suspect they may be in some type of trouble."

"Well, I will put my ear to the streets and see if anyone has any info about your sons or their whereabouts."

"I appreciate that. If something happened to them, I am willing to put up a million dollars to get my sons back."

"Ok Nicolás, I will be in touch."

"Thank you Cristóbal."

Cash hung up the phone and just stared out the window, looking at the warehouse. *A million dollars hitting the streets would make a lot of people talk*, he thought. A war with the Colombians would cripple their organization, if not destroy it. Cash wanted to play chess, not checkers. Each move he made had to be strategic, and he had to be at least two moves ahead of Nicolás.

"What's wrong baby?" Reana asked.

"Nicolás is looking for those fuckin' snakes. He won't stop until he finds out what happened to them."

"Him won't find dem nuh afta Ace drops dem inna dat acid."

"He better not. But this also means we have to get y'all out of here ASAP."

Reana pushed her face up. She had planned to spend a month with Cash before heading back to Jamaica. She didn't expect to cut her visit short. "Yuh wa wi to lef early?"

"Yeah. Y'all need to be out of here by the morning. Ace and your crew are the only ones that know what's going on in that warehouse. Nicolás is going to put pressure on the streets, and I don't want y'all getting caught up in this shit."

"Wi gud at wah wi do. Wi ave dun dis hundreds of times an neva been catch. Wah makes yuh tink wi get catch dis time?" she asked. Anger still masked her face.

"I'm not saying you will. I am just making sure I don't leave any loose ends."

"Wi nuh loose ends wi professionals."

"I know y'all are, but I have to make sure. Just make sure y'all are gone by tomorrow and hit me up when you get back home."

"Wah bout us? Mi miss yuh. Yuh ago cum to Jamaica an visit me?"

"You know I will, as soon as I can." He leaned forward and kissed her, ensuring that he gently bit her plump bottom lip. As soon as he did, Reana flinched. She smiled because Cash knew exactly what that did to her.

Two things turned Reana on, Cash and taking a life. She was like a Black Widow, beautiful but dangerous. The thought of the Muñoz Cartel looking for her crew made her lace panties wet. She lived life on the wild side, and if it weren't for Cash, she would have stayed in Atlanta and welcomed the war. Reana was a lioness that enjoyed to hunt and thirsted for blood. Cash didn't realize that he unleashed a beast in Atlanta and she would soon need to quench her thirst.

# Chapter 17

"Bossman," a young man yelled out.

"Right here," Don said as he walked up to the counter to get his carved ham breakfast sandwich and Frappuccino. The Starbucks employee laughed as he handed Don the order. Customers always left funny names or phrases on their order receipts, but the boy was familiar with Don. Although it had been months since he saw Don in the store, the employee couldn't forget the man who always paid for his meal with a hundred-dollar bill and always told him to keep the change.

"Long time no see," the young boy stated.

"Yes it has been, but I'm back now," Don replied while handing the boy a crisp hundred-dollar bill.

The boy's eyes lit up when he saw the money. "Thank you so much."

Don sat down at the table and placed his breakfast next to his laptop. He scrolled down on the webpage he was checking out. *This would be a nice property to grab*, he thought as he reviewed the building specs. Being incarcerated gave Don the inspiration he needed to want to go completely legit. He had acquired the group millions of dollars' worth of commercial and residential properties. It was now time to elevate their hustle and start looking to acquire open land that would eventually be built on, and they could bring in extra cash from the commercial buildings that would be built on the land. If his plan worked, the crew could retire after a few years and dabble in the real estate business. Without Trey in the way, he was pretty sure he could convince Cash and Ace to get out the coke game.

"So why do they call you Bossman?" a woman asked from behind Don.

He turned and immediately locked on to her hazel eyes. It was as if she was Medusa and turned him to stone. He was still, and he didn't move or speak. The smooth bachelor usually didn't have an issue conversing with an attractive young woman but for some reason, the beauty that stood behind him had him stuck.

"So are you going to tell me why they call you Bossman?" she asked again.

"H-h-hey, I'm Don," he stuttered nervously.

"Can I sit with you, Don?"

"Of course." Don had always dated friends of the women Cash and Ace brought around. They always clowned him for being such a "good guy." Don wasn't the type to run around with different women. He always searched for Mrs. Right but had yet to find her. That was up until he laid eyes on the caramel toned woman that was dressed in a fitted black business suit. Her hair was brushed back in a long ponytail and had blonde highlights. Her French tip, manicured nails also caught his attention because he was a very detailed man. She sat down in the chair next to him and took a sip of her Peppermint Mocha Latte.

"Can I ask you a question?"

"Maybe," she replied jokingly.

"What do you think about this property?" Don slid his laptop over to the woman, and she immediately scrolled up to look at the pictures on the site. He admired her beauty, but he wanted to see where her head was at. Don wanted more than a physical connection with a woman and although she was gorgeous, he knew pretty women came a dime a dozen. The property would surely be impressive to his new associate and the five hundred thousand price tag would let her know why he was called "Bossman." Her finger tapped the "down arrow" key on the keyboard. She was focused on the boatload of information she was viewing on the screen.

"Hmmm."

"Hmmm, what?" Don asked, wondering what she was referring to.

"The property is ok, but for thirty thousand more you could get this building on Metropolitan Park. You might have to put in a little more work to rehab the building, but the lot size is more than double the property in College Park." She slid the laptop back over to Don, and he inspected the property she pulled up on the screen. He didn't say much while looking at the specs, but she knew he was impressed. It seemed as if he was shocked when she mentioned the second property. Now it was her time to admire him. Although Don was involved in risky business, he dressed as if he belonged on the cover of a GQ magazine. His dark chocolate, brown skin was smooth, and his dark goatee was neatly trimmed. He had medium-length curly hair on the top of his head and faded on the back and sides. He was perfect in her eyes. She examined his left hand, and there was no sign of a wedding ring, so she had to make a move on the handsome bachelor.

"It was nice meeting you Don, but I have to head out. I have a busy day ahead of me," she claimed.

"Well, what time should I pick you up tonight for dinner?"

She laughed at how blunt he was. "Who said I was going to dinner with you?"

"Well, since you skipping out on breakfast, I figured we could get more acquainted over a nice steak."

She smiled and handed Don her phone. He wasted no time punching in his digits. He thought about calling his phone to get her number but judging by the way she was undressing him with her eyes, she would surely be calling him. He handed her back the phone and caressed her hand as he pulled his back. Just that subtle touch sent a slight chill up her spine.

"Hit me up later and tell me where to pick you up from."

"Will do." She stood up from the seat and began walking out of the store.

"Wait!" Don yelled out, stopping her before she exited the door. "You never told me your name."

"Ayanna, my name is Ayanna."

# Chapter 18

Cash sat in the hot tub and watched as Reana walked toward him from the bedroom. She looked like she belonged on a runway during fashion week. Her dreads were pulled up into a bun, and Cash couldn't help but stare at her gorgeous face. She could have clearly been a model if she didn't enjoy life as a killer so much. The white, lace lingerie she was wearing hugged her curvy figure. Just like with murder, she enjoyed the process of getting to the climax. She was a tease. Cash reached to the edge of the hot tub and grabbed the bottle of Sangster's Rum Cream. Reana was always sure to bring him several bottles when she flew back and forth. He poured the delicious beverage over four ice cubes and continued watching his beauty.

The tune "After All" by Alkaline was blaring from a wireless speaker, and Cash watched Reana wine her hips. The lace panties were almost lost in her round bottom. He licked his lips, knowing how bad he wanted to taste her. Her smile was nothing short of intoxicating. If Cash's body weren't submerged in the bubbly water, she would see that he was rock hard. He was now on his third glass of the rum cream and leaned forward to watch Reana remove her bra. His mouth dropped as soon as he saw her perky breasts. *So fuckin' flawless.*

"Come here," Cash said. He couldn't take it anymore and wanted to be inside of Reana. She giggled and continued dancing. She was now bent over at the waist, twerking. Each cheek bounced to the rhythm of the music as if her body was synced with the song. Reana looked back at Cash while she was shaking her ass. His eyes were locked on her, and he was finishing the bottle of rum cream. She turned back around and continued twerking, allowing both cheeks to clap together like a round of applause.

Reana felt her head jerk back. Her bun had been unraveled, and her dreads were being pulled. A hand was pushing her shoulders down, keeping her bent at the waist. A wet finger slid her panties to the side and she felt herself being entered. She was so wet and with each stroke, she knew she was leaving the large shaft soaked. Cash wasn't a very patient man and didn't feel like being teased anymore. He rotated his hips and pushed upward, making sure he was stroking at an angle. With each pump, Reana screamed to the top her lungs.

"Oh shit baby, right there!"

Her moans echoed through each room in the mansion and her ass cheeks slapped against his wet body. The fast-paced rhythm began to slow down, and Reana's body began shaking. It was too good. Cash stepped back, allowing his rod to make its way out of her love box slowly. It was dripping, and her legs were still shaking.

"Yuh say yuh want mi to lef, but yuh making mi wa fi stay."

Cash didn't respond. He smirked and walked toward the weakened goddess that he left vulnerable. Her eyes worked their way up and down, scanning his chocolate body. Cash was stocky. At approximately two hundred and twenty pounds, his muscles poked out from every area. His biceps bulged and large veins poked through the skin. He had the strength of an ox, which was displayed when he wrapped his arms around Reana's waist and lifted her off the ground.

"Now you know I wish you could stay, but I have to protect you," he whispered in her ear.

Reana looked into his eyes and melted in his huge arms. She didn't want to leave, but knew the risks she would be taking if the Colombians found out that her crew was responsible for the beating and kidnapping of the Muñoz brothers during a drug transaction. Reana and the Dread Headz crew arranged the meeting through Ramir and posed as dealers from New York. The Muñoz brothers allowed their greed to make them sloppy. They met the Dread Headz in a parking lot and were ambushed during the transaction.

"What you thinking bout?" Cash asked, realizing Reana was in a daze.

"Huh? Nothing," she replied. "Mi cya aks yaah question?"

"Of course you can."

"Yuh love me?"

"You know I do."

Cash lifted her in the air and slid his rod back into her box. "Oh shit," she moaned, not expecting him to manhandle her in such a manner. He walked toward the hot tub, using his strength to balance his lover. With each step he took, she felt him sliding in and out and couldn't help but release more of her love juices all over him. Cash stepped into the hot tub, without loosening his grip. Reana squirmed when she felt the warm water touch her ass. Cash sat back, and she continued mounting him.

"Oh shit," he muttered as the combination of Reana riding him and the soothing warm water made him reach his peak. "Damn baby, I'm 'bout to cum."

"Cum inside mi," she moaned. As soon as the words left her mouth, Cash exploded inside of her warm vagina. Reana continued riding him, as she reached another climax. "Mi love yuh!" she yelled out, wrapping her arms around him and squeezing as hard as she could.

After all the excitement, the couple was exhausted. Reana climbed off her mate and began lightly splashing the bubbles that floated on top the water. Cash sank into the love-filled water and admired his beauty. The last thing he wanted was for something bad to happen to her. His cool and calm demeanor masked the savage that was buried deep inside of him. Blood would stain the streets if anyone laid a finger on his queen.

# Chapter 19

"How much evidence do we need to get a conviction?" Ayanna asked while holding her phone to her ear.

"We need a full confession. There is no other way to link them to the coke that is spreading through the streets. For God's sake, if the Feds couldn't hold them with all the evidence they had compiled. What makes you think we can? We have to work twice as hard as them," Detective Knowles said.

"I need more than just evidence. I have to catch them in the act."

"Do what you have to do. This case will make or break your career. Sergeant Packard was not happy about the bullshit at the homicide scene. He went to our supervisors, and there is chatter that they may be transferring you out of Major Crimes."

"Transferring me out? For what? All because I wanted to investigate the shooting? That's ridiculous."

"You already know how all this political bullshit works."

"Yeah and I know your ass didn't have my back out there either."

"Listen, Ayanna; I have a family that I have to take care of. I don't want to have a career that I am blackballed in. You know what happens when you are thrown to the wolves. You get no chance at promotions, no transfers and the other cops don't back you up. I have worked too hard to deal with that bullshit."

"And you also took an oath, an oath to enforce the law and to have integrity."

"I know the oath that I took."

"Exactly and you know how to investigate. All signs at that crime scene pointed to the Street Kings. You know it did."

"I don't know anything."

"What about the card in the mouth. That's the signature of Corey King."

"But it's not the same card. He was the King of Clubs."

"It doesn't matter. His son could have taken over the legacy and now uses his dad's signature. That is why the Feds picked him. They knew he was responsible for all those murders."

"Then why did the murders continue even when all three of them were locked up?'

"I don't know."

"Exactly. You don't know, and you're only assuming."

"My intuition never lets me down."

"Your intuition? The same intuition that has you obsessed with these men?"

"Yup. Hey listen, I have to go. I'm going to call you tomorrow."

"Ok."

Ayanna watched as the BMW 650 pulled up to the front of Atlas, a luxury restaurant that was draped in elegance. She was wearing a red top, black skirt, a black blazer, and black heels. Her outfit was subtle but sexy. The top was low cut which displayed her cleavage and the skirt was fitted which showed off her curves. Don exited the BMW and handed the key fob to the valet. He was dressed to impress and styled in none other than the crew's signature colors—black and gold. Don was dressed in a tailored-suit from HKT Custom Clothiers. The black shirt and suit served as the backdrop for the gold Cuban links that were draped around his neck.

"Good evening, beautiful," Don greeted.

"Hello, Don."

"You look absolutely stunning."

"I can say the same about you. I see you came red carpet ready." Ayanna tried her best not to show it, but she was enthralled with Don. She had never been on a date with a man of his caliber. He was a young,

# CL LOWRY

handsome, black millionaire. Despite the source of his fortune, no one could deny his ability to negotiate with some of the most prominent business people in the city.

"Shall we?" he asked while holding the door for his beautiful date.

*He is such a gentleman*, she thought. "Yes, we shall."

Don trailed behind Ayanna as the hostess escorted them to their table. Once she got to the table and turned to get a good look at the couple, she couldn't help but to focus on Don. "Please let me know if there is anything you need," she muttered directly to Don. If looks could kill, Ayanna would have been charged with first-degree murder the way she was looking at the hostess. This was a first for Ayanna. Two minutes into their date and Don was being hit on by random women. If they weren't commenting on his chic style, they were staring from across the room.

"Does this happen a lot?" Ayanna asked.

"Does what happen a lot?"

"Women throwing themselves at you."

No, I must say it doesn't."

"For some reason, I find that very hard to believe."

Don grinned and began removing the silverware from the napkin. "Look at this view," he stated, in an effort to change the subject.

"It's beautiful."

"Just like you."

Ayanna blushed. Who would have thought such a simple line would have her head over heels. The small things fascinated her. Things such as holding the doors, checking in on her, and asking her how her day went. Those were the things that made her happy, and Don was already on the right track. Nothing about his demeanor would lead you to believe he was involved in a major drug operation. He was charming, intelligent, and very well versed in the world of real estate.

"So what took you so long to hit me up? I thought you were never going to call."

"Well, I had to make sure you weren't crazy."

"Crazy? Yeah right, says the woman who approaches random people in Starbucks," he said while chuckling.

"No, no, no. I only approach random people in Starbucks that put 'Bossman' on their receipts."

Don couldn't help but laugh. He was in the company of a woman that was not only beautiful but had a sense of humor. The server approached and took their order. Ayanna allowed Don to order her meal as she headed to the bathroom to freshen up. She had always heard raving reviews about the restaurant, but could never afford to eat there. She was mesmerized by the large chandeliers that hung from the ceilings on each level of the restaurant. Ayanna even considered the bathroom fancy with the restroom attendant handing her a warm towel to wipe her hands after washing them. After returning from the bathroom, she saw the server pouring two glasses of wine.

"What kind of wine is this?" Ayanna asked as she sat back down at the table.

"2005 Châteaud' Yquem, 1er Grand Cru Supérieur, Sauternes, Bordeaux," the server replied.

"Wow. That sounds expensive."

"It's $200 a glass," the server said before heading away from the table.

"Don, $200 is a lot of money for some wine."

"Taste it," Don responded.

Ayanna looked at him as if he was crazy. He smiled at her then nodded his head. She raised the glass, and the aroma of the beverage grabbed her interest. She placed her full lips on the glass and then tilted it, allowing the wine to pour into her mouth slowly. "Oh wow, that is smooth."

"Only the best for the best."

The server returned with a plethora of appetizers. Ayanna had not been on a date in years and had never been on one so luxurious. Don was already spoiling her, and she felt a bit awkward as the server refilled their wine glasses. *That's almost a thousand dollars in wine.* The Georgia Peach Panzanella danced on Ayanna's taste buds. Don and Ayanna were both diving into the appetizers when the server brought out two steak entrées, a rack of lamb and salmon. The date was amazing to Ayanna. They laughed, ate well, and enjoyed each other's company. After the perfect date, it was time to leave, and Ayanna headed back to Don's condo. She started the night out in investigation mode, but after such an amazing dinner, the investigation was the last thing on her mind.

As soon as Don opened the front door, they began knocking items down. They were all over each other, kissing, licking, rubbing, grabbing, squeezing, and more. They worked their way to the bedroom and straight to the bed. Don's hands explored her body. The smoothness of her skin guided his hands around the surface of her body. His hands roamed up her shirt and cupped her soft breasts. He immediately worked his hands to her back and unclasped her bra. Don was slow and sensual. Each touch was soft and as Ayanna's body was revealed, he worshipped every part of it. Most men that have been locked up for a significant period of time would have devoured Ayanna, but Don took his time. Just like a lion watching its prey, Don waited for the perfect opportunity to strike. Ayanna didn't expect things to get this far so soon, but she knew the risks of going undercover. Many detectives have used drugs, committed crimes, and engaged in sexual activity to prevent their covers from being blown. She wanted to take the Street Kings down so bad that she was willing to sleep with each one of them if it meant she would gain access into their circle.

Ayanna moaned as Don's hands were now roaming up her legs. She was getting wet and loved his touch. She didn't want this moment to end. Soon, his hands were gripping her firm ass and her body was begging him to have his way. Ayanna couldn't take it anymore. She wanted him. She pushed Don back into the center of the plush California king bed and began undressing him. She removed his Hermes belt and unbuckled his slacks. As soon as she pulled the slacks down to his ankles, she saw what he was working with.

"Oh shit," she muttered under her breath as she laid eyes on his large, thick penis.

Ayanna immediately knew it would be too much for her to handle. She hadn't been in a serious relationship in over a year and hadn't had sex in eight months. Don's large rod would surely tear down her walls.

Don pulled Ayanna close and began kissing her soft lips. His warmth engulfed her, causing Ayanna to melt in his arms. The two rolled around the bed making out and ripping the rest of each other's clothes off. Suddenly Don's two hundred pound frame had mounted her curvy body. He spread her legs and slowly entered her vagina, which was soaking wet.

"Oh fuck," Ayanna moaned once she felt Don stretching her walls.

She wrapped her arms around his neck and kept his body close to hers. They were sharing their warmth, and she was enjoying every inch he was sliding in her. Their lips locked and Don plunged deeper and deeper. Ayanna had completely forgotten about her mission and was enjoying the ecstasy she was feeling. Ayanna looked into Don's eyes as he pleased her. A single tear ran down her cheek due to the guilt she felt. She was only using him and planned to put him behind bars, and he was here allowing her to enjoy his company and body.

"Damn, right there. Right there," she yelled out, feeling her body reach its peak. Seconds later, her body released her love juices all over his shaft as he continued stroking. "What are you doing to me?" Ayanna asked. No man had ever touched or fucked her the way Don was.

"I'm lovin' you, baby," he replied, causing her body to immediately shake and release once more.

The wetness made him speed up his stroke as he felt a rush of pleasure shooting through his body. He pulled his dick out of her love pool and ejaculated on her stomach. It was warm and runny. Don collapsed on top of Ayanna and wrapped his arms around her. The couple was exhausted, and they were both sound asleep in minutes. It was a night to remember.

# Chapter 20

It was about four in the morning, and Don was still sleeping. Ayanna sat up and just watched him. He looked so innocent in her eyes. She was confused. A part of her wanted to slap cuffs on him at that moment, and another part of her wanted to get to know him more. Everyone in Atlanta knew about the Street Kings and how they made their money. It was no secret that they were supplying most of Atlanta with cocaine. After they were released from federal custody, the Major Crimes Unit wanted nothing to do with the Street Kings. There was going to be a huge lawsuit being filed against the Feds, and the last thing Atlanta PD wanted was the suit to focus on them. Anytime someone beat a federal case there is no way a local department would have enough to bring up charges. This is precisely why Ayanna wanted to bring a case against them; it was a challenge she wanted to accept. Despite having very little support from other detectives in her unit, she was determined to bring down a big name in the streets. A successful investigation against the Street Kings would make Ayanna first in line for a promotion. She thought she was going to hook up with a thug and get him to confess to being a cocaine distributor. Little did she know the Street Kings were a three-headed monster and none of them was like the other. Don's only connection to the drugs was the cash he invested into properties. He had no dealings with the drug shipments or transactions. Ayanna snuck out the bedroom and snooped through the luxurious condo. She opened drawers, checked the freezer and closets, but there was no sign of drugs or any other illegal activity. Judging by the way his residence was set up, you couldn't tell Don was involved in the drug game at all. There were photos of his family, including Cash and his uncle, Corey. The more Ayanna looked around the condo, the more she began liking Don even more. Her investigation quickly switched to infatuation. She stumbled upon a large painting that was displayed over an electric fireplace. It was a large, hand-painted image of four playing cards—**THE KING OF HEARTS, KING OF DIAMONDS, KING OF CLUBS AND KING OF SPADES.**

"Yo, what are you doing?" Don asked as he emerged from his bedroom.

"Who is this?" Ayanna asked, holding a photo of Corey King. She knew who he was but wanted to hear Don's response.

Don walked up to Ayanna and looked over her shoulder at the framed photograph. "That's my uncle."

"Were you two close?"

"Yup. My dad died when I was young, so my uncle was basically my father figure. He is the reason why I got into real estate business."

"Oh, so he is a realtor?"

"Nope. He was actually a drug dealer. It was the only way he knew how to survive, and that was only a stepping-stone in his life. Later on, he got out the drug game and bought a bunch of clubs. Then one day he was murdered. Someone shot him and burned his body."

"Oh my god, that's horrible. I'm sorry to hear that." She was surprised Don was so honest about his uncle.

"Yeah, I know that his death wasn't random. Someone targeted him, and I think it had something to do with his past. The demons he thought he left when he got out the drug game must have caught up to him."

"Did they ever find out who did it?"

"Did what?"

"Killed your uncle. Did the police ever find his killer?"

"The police?" Don chuckled. "Fuck the police. I doubt they even looked for a killer. They don't care about us, and I know they aren't investigating the murders of black people, especially not a black man that was a former drug dealer."

Ayanna got pissed at Don's blatant disrespect for her career choice but didn't want her emotions to show. She placed the photograph back on the shelf and turned toward Don. He was much different from what she expected. She was sure that he would hide the fact that he was the nephew of one of the biggest drug dealers in Atlanta, but he didn't. He was honest and caring. They were both in their underwear and were approving of each other's physiques. Ayanna rubbed her hand across Don's bulky chest. She hadn't realized just how sexy he was during the activities the prior night. Don didn't have a ripped body, but he had mass. He was solid and strong. Ayanna couldn't help but stare at his thick dick print, which protruded through his Calvin Klein briefs. Although her plan wasn't to stay this long at his place, she wanted to feel him inside of her once more. Her love button was throbbing, and he had what she needed to satisfy the urge.

Ayanna grabbed Don's package and pulled him close to her. Her aggression turned him on, and his print was now stiff. He sat on the sectional and pulled her on top of him, displaying his strength. Her panties were now moist. Don slid his rod out his briefs and used the head to push Ayanna's wet panties to the side. As soon as he entered her, she screamed seductively. Her nails dug into his back, and with each thrust, she slowly scratched him. The slight pain got Don excited, and he continued to grind his hips. Ayanna had no control, and his strength became unbearable. She didn't want to reach her climax so soon, but every move he made was perfect. After spending those months in prison, Don had a ton of aggression to release. Their first encounter was sensual, but this time he was ready to show off.

Don stood to his feet. Ayanna still straddled his rod and wrapped her arms around his neck to prevent from falling. Don palmed both of her ass cheeks and squeezed tightly, locking Ayanna in place. He sunk his teeth into her shoulder, almost breaking the skin, and began thrusting. Ayanna went crazy. Her moans sounded more like screams, as she felt the fast and deep strokes. More scratches appeared on Don's back as Ayanna attempted to keep her grip. She tried locking her legs around him to make him slow down, but his pace increased. He was a beast that couldn't be tamed. His teeth had now sunk into her neck, as his fast stroke sped up. "I'm about to cum," she moaned before hopping off his rod. She was so unsteady on her feet. Her legs wobbled as a warm liquid dripped from her vagina. Ayanna was done, but Don wasn't.

He grabbed her by the waist and whispered, "Turn around."

Don placed his hand on the small of her back and reintroduced his thick cock to her love box. The head to his cock stretched her to new limits.

"Damn baby," she moaned, as she felt every inch slide in and out of her.

Don gripped her ass while he stroked. Ayanna could barely stand. She was bent over the arm of the sectional, so her legs didn't have to do much work. She was still shaking. With every stroke, Don's balls slapped against her throbbing clit. Ayanna bit into the couch pillow to prevent her from blaring in pleasure.

"You like that, baby?" Don asked, although he already knew the answer. The muffled response indicated that Ayanna was enjoying every second. He continued stroking, slapping her plump ass in between thrusts.

"I'm about to cum again," Ayanna yelled out, knowing she couldn't resist his loving. She buried her face in the sectional as she let out a loud shriek. Just as she reached her peak, she felt a warm fluid filling her box.

"Grrr, fuck," Don grunted as he came inside of Ayanna. It felt too good to pull out.

"That was so good," she said. "You are so good."

Don smiled. He sat on the sectional and pulled Ayanna onto his lap. Despite him ejaculating inside her, his penis was still large when it wasn't fully erect. She felt it pressed up against her ass cheek and he felt his semen escaping her vagina. Ayanna felt Don's huge arms encompass her body and rested her head on his shoulder.

"I don't want to leave," she whispered in his ear.

"You don't have to." Ayanna smiled and sunk into his arms. "I have plans for later if you're free."

"What time?" she asked.

"All night."

Her smile had now spread from ear to ear. It seemed as if Don knew all the right things to say to her. She hadn't ever been with a man of his stature. He was the complete opposite of what she expected, and now he had let her into his world. Ayanna looked over at the family portrait and the painting of the playing cards. She was in too deep.

# Chapter 21

The lights in the nightclub were flashing, and the music was blasting throughout the building. The club nearly reached capacity as the crowd continued flowing in. Everyone attended the celebration of Don's birthday. From beautiful women to Atlanta's biggest moneymakers, no one wanted to miss a party thrown by the Street Kings. The DJ spun the hottest hip-hop tunes and shouted out Don from the moment the doors opened. Every seat at the bar was filled, and the bartenders were mixing drink after drink. "It's so lit in here tonight," the DJ announced. "Y'all already know we are here celebrating Don's birthday, so make sure y'all show him so love. The Street Kings are in the building."

Don stood in the VIP section, overseeing the entire party. The section was large and included six sectionals, six tables, a private bar, and a host of servers. Five smaller VIP sections also circled the balcony of the nightclub. They were filled with entertainers, athletes, and millionaire business owners that wanted to show off alongside street royalty. Don admired the layout of the building, which was modern and unlike any other club in the country. Don felt like a god amongst men from his vantage point. "How's the view?" Cash asked.

"This is amazing. How did you find this place?"

"I had to find the perfect gift for my cousin's birthday."

"Well, this party is a great gift. You already know I'm a low-key guy so this is beyond anything that I could put together."

"Party? The party isn't your gift. The club is."

"Get the fuck out of here!" Don yelled in disbelief. He gave Cash a tight hug before returning to the balcony and overseeing the party once more. "Yo Ace, you knew about this?"

"Hell yeah, birthday boy. You aren't the only one who can buy up property," Ace replied. He leaned forward, grabbed his bottle of Ace of Spades, and took a swig. Ace was relaxing on one of the sectionals with Ramir and four women that could easily be supermodels. Ace sprinkled a small pile of cocaine on the table and watched as the women cut lines and vacuumed the drug with their nostrils. The Street Kings were notorious for throwing the most lavish parties in Atlanta and this night would be no different.

"Mr. King, your guest has arrived," one of the bouncers announced.

Everyone stopped when she walked into the section. The tight yellow dress hugged every curve of her body. Her shoulder-length kinky curls bounced as she strutted toward her man. Don's mouth dropped to the floor when he spotted Ayanna walking toward him. Ace and Ramir paid the women by their sides no mind as the lights glistened off Ayanna's deep brown skin.

"Wow, look at you," Don said. He gave Ayanna a big hug, lifting her off the ground. It took him a while to get through to her but she made him happy, and he felt as if his life was complete with her by his side.

"Happy Birthday, baby," Ayanna whispered in his ear before placing her thick, moist lips on his.

"Whoa, whoa, whoa. You must be the woman my cousin can't stop talking about," Cash said, interrupting the couple's intimate greeting.

Ayanna looked over and seemed a bit startled when she saw Cash. She saw pictures of him in Don's condo, but it was much different when she was face to face with the son of the man she hunted for years. A part of her wished she could arrest him on the spot and embarrass him in front of the entire crowd, but she remembered the outcome of the federal case they beat. She knew the only chance she had at getting Cash behind bars was to gain his trust and infiltrate the organization.

"Hi, I'm Ayanna."

"It's so nice to meet you, Ayanna. Did my cousin tell you the great news yet?" Cash said while shaking her hand.

"What great news?"

"You are standing in my new nightclub," Don stated.

"What? That is wonderful news. Congratulations baby." Ayanna placed another soft kiss on Don's lips.

"Thanks, baby. Cash got it for me as a birthday gift."

"Wow, that's one heck of a gift."

"Yeah, I wanted it to be a surprise for him. So what are your plans with my cousin?" Cash asked.

"What do you mean?"

"Well, he is a great guy, and I just want to make sure he finds the right woman that can make him happy and be loyal to him."

Ayanna looked around, noticing the other women in the section. "Well I wonder if the same rule applies to everyone in here," she countered, referring to the women using drugs, drinking their faces away, and throwing themselves at members of the organization.

Cash also looked around and laughed. "Well, Donny here is different. He is one of the good ones, and he deserves a good one. As you see, we have plenty of women that are just here for a come up."

"Well I am a good one, and Donovan knows that I don't want anything from him except for his heart."

"And you got it," Don added. He kissed her on the forehead and held her hand.

The couple walked to one of the sectionals and sat down. One of the servers came over and poured them both a glass of white wine. Don's happiness was written all over his face, and Ayanna felt the same joy. Butterflies fluttered in her stomach every time he kissed her forehead. With each day that passed, it became more difficult to focus on her task. Don was the complete opposite of what she imagined he would be and at that moment, she noticed Cash was too. He was walking around the section mingling but paid no attention to the thirsty women that seemed to be throwing themselves at him. He was very aware of his surroundings and kept an eye on everyone, including Ayanna.

As the party continued, Cash never drank anything but water. Ayanna pictured him to be a reckless showoff that wanted to flaunt his money, but it seemed that only Ace had that mentality. Ayanna continued drinking wine and pretended to take selfies as she snapped photos of each person that was partying with the Street Kings. Testimony alone would mean nothing when trying to build a criminal case against the powerhouse organization.

As time continued, the club became more packed, and it was time for the actual celebration of Don's birthday. "Come on y'all, we hittin' the floor," Cash announced to the entire section. The Street Kings and all their guests made their way downstairs led by Cash. Once he hit the edge of the dance floor, he moved aside and allowed Don to step forward. With Ayanna on his arm, the couple stepped forward and saw the path of servers that were holding up large bottles of champagne with sparklers attached. The pathway was lit up and led to the center of the dance floor. It was an entrance fit for a king—a STREET KING.

Ayanna was in awe as she walked side by side with Don. Being with him opened her up to an entirely different lifestyle that was far more luxurious and exciting than hers. The more time she spent with Don, the more she fell for him. She liked the spotlight and all the attention that came with the relationship, especially because no one on the police force paid her any attention. Deep down inside the thought of leaving the force and being with Don crossed her mind.

"Here comes the birthday boy," the DJ broadcasted.

Flashes from cameras, cheers from the crowd, and the support of his friends made Don feel like he was on the top of the world. As he approached the center of the dance floor, he thought about the jail cell he recently spent months in. Freedom used to be something he took for granted but after having it stripped away from him, he appreciated every second. That feeling expanded into his need to find someone to share the rest of his life with, which explained the bulge in his pocket. The ring box in his pocket was noticeable, but he kept his suit jacket on which left it partially covered. Ayanna never noticed the bulge and had no idea Don was ready to propose to her just after a short time after being together.

The couple reached the center of the dance floor where the servers brought out a large birthday cake. The cake was rolled out on a table and had to be at least five feet high. The majority of the cake was covered in white buttercream icing, but it was decorated in black and gold icing as well.

"This is one hell of a party, cuz," Don said.

"You deserve it, man," Cash replied while handing Don a solid gold cake knife.

The cheers from the crowd continued as Don approached his cake. The entire club erupted as he dug the knife into the cake and made the first slice. Don was smiling from ear to ear, soaking up the moment, and enjoying all the positive vibes being sent his way. It was now the perfect time to secure his fate with Ayanna. He looked back at her and was immediately sucked into her beauty. She seemed happy, which made him happy. Don slowly reached into his pocket and grabbed the ring box. He turned around to drop on one knee...*BANG!*

*BANG! BANG! BANG!*

The gunshots made the crowd scatter like roaches. People were screaming and trampling over each other, trying to make it to the exits. Cash reached for his waistband, where he usually kept a gun tucked. He didn't even realize he was formally dressed and never tucked his strap. None of the crew was strapped because they hired security for the party.

"You motherfuckas' have some nerve," a voice said.

Cash and the other Street Kings watched as Antonio and two other members of his crew advanced on them with guns pointed in their direction. Ramir looked over at Ace and knew what this charade was over.

"Y'all clowns think y'all were gonna' kill my little brother and then throw a fuckin' party," Antonio yelled. Saliva flew from his mouth with every word he spoke. Rage covered his face and flames shot from his eyes.

"What the fuck are you talkin' about Tone?" Cash asked.

Tone had a firm grip on his gun with his right hand and reached into his back pocket with his left. "This was left on my brother's dead body," Antonio said, throwing the bloody playing card at Cash.

Cash looked at the card and glanced over at Ace. He knew things on the street were handled, but there was a certain way things needed to be done. When attacking an organization, the strongest link needed to be taken out and that was Antonio. He should have been the main target, not Los. Cash kicked the card back toward Antonio. "Tone, you don't want to do this."

"Shut the fuck up," Antonio barked, letting off a shot in the air. There were screams and pleading, but nothing was going to change Antonio's mind. The men he stood before were responsible for his family's grief and pain. Nothing could bring Los back, but Antonio had nothing else to lose. His finger danced around the trigger as he lowered his gun, pointing it directly in Cash's face. "You killed Los and now I'm going to kill every last one of you motherfuckas'."

"Atlanta Police, drop your weapon."

The sound of the woman's voice immediately grabbed Antonio's attention and the Glock that was pointed at him kept his attention. Antonio kept a firm grip on his gun. His eyes were looking at the Glock, but his gun was still pointed at Cash.

*BANG! BANG!*

Cash and the others couldn't believe it. Once the shots were fired, everyone took off running. Antonio dropped to his knees. The two shots that were fired from the Glock ripped through his chest and shoulder. Ayanna watched Antonio drop his gun and place his hands over the two entrance wounds. Antonio's goons couldn't make any moves before guns were pressed against the back of their heads. More shots were let off, and the two goons were executed right beside Antonio. Brain matter and blood covered the center of the dance floor.

Ayanna glanced over the panicking crowd but was unable to locate the executors among the remaining crowd. She turned around to check on Don, but there was no trace of him or any of the other Street Kings. The women that previously were enjoying their company were still on location. Some were face down on the ground, and others headed for the front door with the remaining crowd. It was pure commotion in the club.

Ayanna attempted to push her way through the crowd, in an effort to locate the two shooters. Her petite frame bounced off shoulders as she maintained a tight grip on her handgun. The flashing strobe lights made it difficult to get a good look at the shooters, who were wearing black hoodies when they executed Antonio's goons. Ayanna continued pushing through the crowd until she made her way out the club. With her gun raised, she scanned the crowd. Focusing on everyone's hands, Ayanna tried her best to locate the gunmen but to no avail.

Multiple cars were speeding up and down the street, but it was impossible for Ayanna to know if any of them were related to the shooters. She was in a very vulnerable spot, standing in front of the club. It was an amusing sight, seeing this beautiful woman in a tight dress waving a gun around. Although most of the patrons were leaving the scene, some were mingling on the sidewalk with their cell phones out, recording video of the incident. Ayanna made her way back into the club, which was now empty besides the three bodies on the dance floor.

"Hello this is Detective Ali," Ayanna said after dialing 911 on her cell phone. "I'm at the corner of McDaniel Street and Ralph David Abernathy

Boulevard. There has been a shooting at a nightclub. We have three gunshot victims, so please send out paramedics, and I'm going to need back up out here."

Ayanna walked up to the first goon and placed two fingers on the inside of his wrist. No pulse. She checked the second goon. No pulse. She grabbed Antonio's limp wrist, checking for a pulse. The throbbing of the radial artery surprised her. She turned his body over and immediately noticed he was unresponsive. The front of his shirt was drenched in blood. Fearing he would bleed out, Ayanna scanned the club for something that could be useful to her. She spotted the hand towels at the bar and snatched them up. She folded one of the towels and placed it over the gushing wound on Antonio's chest. The towel soaked up the blood in seconds as she pushed the towel against the wound.

The sound of sirens echoed in the distance. Minutes felt like hours as Ayanna did her best to keep Antonio alive. *Why the hell would you come here tonight? This was a suicide mission*, she thought. Ayanna needed answers, and she wasn't going to allow the one person with those answers to die in her arms. Antonio could be the key to putting the Street Kings behind bars. If he was crazy enough to attempt to kill them in their own club, he would surely be willing to testify against the crew and put them all away.

The front door of the club flung open as several police officers and detectives filed into the club.

"Over here!" Ayanna yelled.

One of the officers led the paramedics to Ayanna and Antonio. They wasted no time working on him and preparing him for transport. Another pair of paramedics checked the other two bodies and confirmed the obvious. They were dead.

# Chapter 22

"Yo, what the fuck?" Cash yelled as the driver sped off from the club. The Street Kings were able to dip out through an exit in the VIP section of the club, but that didn't mean they were in the clear just yet. Ayanna was too distracted by Antonio and his goons to notice the Street Kings make their move out of the club. Cash sat in the front seat of the black Cadillac Escalade and scrolled through the contacts in his phone before he began texting. His thumbs were working overtime as he sent out several text messages.

Ace was very fidgety in the back seat as he nervously squirmed around. Ramir sat between Ace and Don in the back seat of the Cadillac. He had never seen his cousin act in this manner, and a part of him was too nervous to ask a question.

"YOU FUCKIN' RAT!" Ace yelled as he pulled a dagger from his ankle and pressed it firmly against

Don's neck. He mugged Ramir out the way to get to his target. The tip of the blade pierced against Don's skin. The small puncture caused a trickle of blood run down the blade.

"Ace, chill," Cash pleaded, knowing it wouldn't take much for Ace to slide the blade across Don's neck.

"Fuck this rat, Cash. He is fuckin' with the cops."

"I didn't know she was a cop. I swear I didn't," Don blurted out. The blade was still pressed against his neck, and he could feel Ace applying more pressure and sliding it deeper into the wound. "Ace, I didn't know she was a damn cop."

"Yes, you did!" Ace barked. Fire was in his eyes as he watched Don cower in fear.

"I said chill! Cash yelled, pressing a Keltec handgun against Ace's temple. For as much as Cash knew what Ace was capable of, Ace knew Cash wouldn't hesitate to protect his family.

"Cash what the fuck are you doing? He is in bed with a fuckin' cop."

"He said he didn't know she was a cop."

"You believe that bullshit? "

"I believe my cousin."

"Just like you believed all that bullshit Trey used to say right? Look how he turned out."

"He ain't Trey, motherfucker."

Despite the gun being pressed against his head, Ace still kept the dagger in place. Cash slid his index finger over the trigger. "Put that fuckin' knife down before I blow your brains all over that backseat."

Ace paused for a moment, and then his eyes sharply cut to the left. He noticed the placement of Cash's finger on the trigger and realized the situation was intensifying. Ace pulled the knife back and released his grip on Don's shirt.

"This is crazy. Pull this fuckin' car over," he demanded, smacking the driver in the back of the head. The driver slammed on the brakes and made an abrupt stop in traffic. As soon as the Cadillac stopped, Ace hopped out, and Ramir followed. "If I find out you're a rat, I'm going to gut you like a fish, motherfucker," Ace said directly to Don.

There was no time to respond before Ace slammed the door and started walking off. Don's hand was up at his neck, checking the severity of the wound. He was still in shock over the entire ordeal.

"Cuz, I'm serious. I didn't know she was a cop."

"I know you didn't. I think Ace knows it too, but you know how he gets."

"He should know I would never say anything. I didn't say a word while we were all locked up, so why would I say something now?"

"You never thought anything was weird about her?"

"Nope. Not at all."

"Where did y'all meet?"

"We met in Starbucks."

"When?"

"As soon as we beat the case." Don shook his head at the irony.

"How serious are y'all?"

"That's my girl, and honestly I'm falling for her. Well, I was falling for her."

"So why wouldn't she just tell you that she's a cop?"

"I don't know. I don't fuckin' know." Don banged his fist on the door panel. Thoughts of him and Ayanna ran through his mind. *Why wouldn't she tell me?*

"We have to figure out what she was doing at the club tonight."

"How the hell are we going to do that? I don't want nothing to do with her, cuz."

"Too bad. If she calls you, you have to play her game. Since her little secret is out now, you gotta find out everything about her and everything she knows about us."

"This is some bullshit."

"I know, but it is what it is," Cash said. He reached back and placed the handgun on Don's lap. "Keep your friends close and your enemies closer."

# Chapter 23

Ayanna stared at her Samsung cell phone. A part of her knew there was nothing of concern in the phone, but that didn't stop her from hoping Don would text or call her. Since the truth had been exposed, she wanted the opportunity to explain herself. Everyone in the department was already skeptical of her undercover operation, and now it looked like she was a shooter for the Street Kings.

"Let me find out you went all Assassin Creed in here," Detective Knowles said jokingly as he approached his partner.

"Naw, I just hit one of these guys. What are you doing here?" she asked.

"I came because I heard you were involved, and I had to come to make sure you were ok."

"I don't need a babysitter, Cliff. I'm a big girl."

"Yes you are," he muttered, admiring how good Ayanna looked in her tight dress. "So what the hell were you doing in here?"

"Now you know that ain't happening."

"What?"

"You know damn well I'm not going to stand here and answer any of your questions." Ayanna paced back and forth. Her focus was on her phone. There was still no word from Don. *I should call him. What if something happened to him?* Ayanna was so worried that she didn't even notice the lead investigator walk in the club.

"Well, well, well, look who it is," Sergeant Packard said once he spotted Ayanna standing in the corner. Ayanna froze as soon as she laid eyes on him. The last person she expected to see was him and after the blow up at the Willis Jamison crime scene, she wasn't ready for round two with Sergeant Packard. "I'm going to make this easy for you," he said as he walked toward her. "Contact your union rep and a private attorney because if I find anything that even looks like it's funny, I'm going to roof you. I'll be in contact with you soon, so have your story straight."

Ayanna was stuck like a deer in headlights. It was hard to believe what she was up against. Sergeant Packard didn't like her and now had his chance to take not only her badge but also her freedom if he wanted. "All I need to know is if you had anything to do with any of these shootings." Ayanna didn't say a word. Her silence answered his question. "Where is your firearm?"

Ayanna opened her purse, exposing the firearm. Sergeant Packard quickly slid a glove on his right hand and reached in the purse to grab his evidence. "Hey, why are you taking my phone? You only need the gun."

"Oh, now you can speak, huh? I'm taking your phone because I know there is going to be something in here that will be interesting to me."

"You're going to need a warrant to get in my phone."

"Trust me, I plan on getting one. You can get the hell out of my crime scene now. I'll be in touch."

Steam blew out of Ayanna's ears as she stormed out of the club. There wasn't much for her to do now but play the waiting game and to see what the investigation would uncover. All she knew was Don deserved an explanation.

Chapter 24

"Where the fuck you been at?" Yvette asked, entering the passenger side of the white Dodge Challenger.

"I've been around," Ramir said, leaning in for a kiss. His lips pressed against Yvette's, causing her to sink into the passenger seat of the vehicle. "Is everything ok?"

"Fuck no, Ramir. My world was flipped upside down, and you were nowhere to be found. I know we just started dating, but I need you right now." A single tear slid down Yvette's face, followed by another. Pain and grief were in each teardrop.

"What's wrong 'ma?"

"My brother got killed," she said, trying to hold back further tears from falling.

"What!? Which brother? When the fuck did this happen?"

"Carlos. They killed him right out here," she replied, pointing to the front of The Cut apartments.

"Damn shawty, sorry for your loss. Do y'all know who killed him?"

"Yeah. You ever heard of the Street Kings?"

"Naw. Who are they?"

"Some bitch ass dudes that think they run this city. Carlos and Antonio used to get drugs from them. I never saw them around here, but they would always talk about them." More tears began coming down. "I can't keep talking about this. I want to take my mind off of it."

Ramir leaned in again and kissed Yvette. This time his hand grazed her breasts before gripping her shoulders and pulling her in close. She hissed, clawing at the seats as Ramir nibbled on her neck. The sudden shine from passing headlights made them both nervous. Ramir looked out his window at the black, tinted out Benz that drove by.

"Let's go inside," Yvette suggested.

Ramir didn't plan to be walking into the devil's mouth. If he stepped foot in The Cut, he would be in the center of the D-Block gang's territory and that would be suicide. Although Yvette didn't know about his affiliation with the Street Kings, that didn't mean someone else wouldn't have recognized him, especially if they were at Don's party when all the drama popped off.

"Let's go somewhere else," Ramir suggested before slamming on the gas pedal and taking off. Ramir turned up the radio and blasted *"I Need You"* by Derez De'Shon. He grabbed the blunt from the center console and sparked it up. He inhaled the herb and blew the smoke in Yvette's face. She smiled and took the blunt out of Ramir's mouth. She was still in mourning over Los' death, so she didn't even consider puffing and passing. She needed it all to keep her mind off her brother's death. She nodded her head to the music, leaned back, and blew the smoke out the cracked window. After finishing the blunt, Yvette flicked the end out the window. She looked over at Ramir, captivated by his handsomeness. He had a fresh cut, his waves were spinning, and she loved the tattoos that decorated his entire body, including his face.

Yvette didn't know most of those tattoos represented the work he put in on the streets. Ramir's coping mechanism was pain. Once he inflicted pain on someone else, he needed the physical pain to take his mind off the death he caused. Tattoos were somewhat of an outlet for him. Yvette never questioned Ramir about what he did. She knew he was in the streets, but didn't know he was running the Street Kings while the heads of the organization were arrested. She didn't know that he had been playing her and used her to get information on Los and Antonio. Their bond helped him orchestrate Los' murder with the help of the Dread Headz. Ramir was subtle and patient, which made him more dangerous than Ace. Ace would have sent a bullet through Yvette's skull the moment he saw her, but Ramir had compassion for her. Although their relationship was built on lies, it was a relationship nonetheless.

Ramir pulled up to a house on Argonne Drive in Buckhead. He pulled into the driveway, and they both exited the Challenger and entered the home. "Whose house is this?" Yvette asked, looking around at the nicely furnished living room.

"It's ours," Ramir said and chuckled.

"Yeah ok." Yvette laughed.

Ramir hugged Yvette from behind and continued what he started in the car. He pulled her hair to the side and started kissing the back of her neck. He knew precisely what she liked. Yvette moaned and gripped the arm of the couch. Her phone began ringing, but she ignored the call and focused on the man that was making her feel good at the moment. Being with Ramir was a temporary relief to her pain. Ramir pulled her shirt over her head, exposing the blue, lace bra that was holding up her large breasts. Yvette was sacred to the D-Block gang. She was supposed to be untouchable, so the mere fact that Ramir had her open was a win in itself. He squeezed her breasts as he began working the kisses down her back. Yvette began moaning louder. Her panties were now soaked, and she wanted them off. She unbuttoned her jeans and quickly dropped them to the floor, along with her panties.

"Make me feel good baby," Yvette moaned before bending over the couch and showing Ramir her goods.

"I got you." Ramir reached in his pocket and ripped open the Magnum condom. He unbuckled his pants and slid the condom on. He slid into Yvette, allowing her moistness to assist him.

"Oh sí, Papi!" Yvette screamed out.

He wasted no time pounding her with hard strokes. Smacking her ass, pulling her hair, and manhandling Yvette like a toy, Ramir sent her into a frenzy of pleasure. Her body began shaking as she exploded on his dick. That didn't stop Ramir from continuing his stroke. Yvette looked back at him. Her brown eyes locked with his as hot pleasure clawed at every inch of their bodies. She bit her lip as Ramir pushed her head further into the couch. His strong hands made it impossible for her to move. She couldn't last as the climax felt as if it were shutting her entire body down. Yvette felt weak.

Ramir continued running his hands all over her body. He exposed her breasts and pinched her nipples as he continued stroking. Yvette went crazy.

"Fuck yeah!" Ramir yelled out as he ejaculated and filled the condom. "I'm sorry baby girl," he whispered in her ear just before pulling out her box.

"Sorry? Sorry for what?"

"Sorry for killing your brother, bitch," Ace said.

Yvette jumped up after hearing the unfamiliar voice. She attempted to cover herself up, seeing that strange men were standing behind Ramir. "What the fuck is going on Ramir?"

"Listen, Yvette. I need to tell you something."

"Who are these guys and why the fuck did he say they killed my brother?" Tears began to pool up in her eyes. It seemed as if they were waiting for the truth to come out before falling.

"Your brothers weren't loyal. They knew they were only supposed to cop weight from us. Once they started going behind our backs to get their work, they violated the rules."

"Us? Who the fuck is us?"

"You know who we are, baby."

"Don't you fuckin' call me baby. What the fuck are you saying, Ramir?"

Ramir didn't expect this moment to be so difficult. He figured telling Yvette the truth would give them both some much-needed closure. He reached into his pocket and pulled out a wad of cash."

"What the fuck is that asshole? What the fuck is that money gon' to do for me?"

Ramir unfolded the wad of cash and unveiled what was buried in between. He removed the item and reached it out to hand to Yvette—**THE JACK OF HEARTS**. Before he knew it, a big glob of spit landed on his nose that was followed up by a hard smack to the face.

"You motherfucker!" Yvette yelled as she began throwing fists at Ramir. She would never forget the card that was left at the scene of her brother's murder. This was confirmation that Ramir was involved. He did his best to block each blow, allowing her to let out her rage. The moment was short-lived, once a right hook from Ace rocked Yvette. She was temporarily caught in a daze as she tried to gather her bearings. Another blow came in the form a swift kick to the face, which knocked two of the front teeth from her mouth and sent her right back into the daze. Ace set up for another blow, but Ramir stood in front of him.

"Chill cuz, I got this. I owe her that much."

"Man, you don't owe this bitch shit!" Ace barked.

"I know, but I gotta be the one to do this."

"Do what?" Yvette muttered before spitting out a large glob of blood.

Ramir leaned down and kissed her on the forehead. "Listen, baby. Antonio came by on some reckless shit and we gotta send a message to the whole city. The Street Kings aren't to be fucked with."

Yvette began weeping. "S—So how you gon' send that message?"

Ramir just looked her. Seeing her bruised up and missing teeth should have been enough to shake up the D-Block gang, but Antonio's actions solidified her grave. "Baby girl, just close your eyes. Things are going to be fine."

"NO! Tell me what you gon' do. You gon' kill me?"

"Family comes first. You know that. Your big brother threatened my family tonight, and we can't let that shit ride. So if you must know, after I kill you I'm going to go through your phone and text your mom and every other member of your family that you're close to. I'm going to kill every one of them. Their bloody bodies will decorate your entire hood."

# Chapter 25

The Cadillac pulled up directly in front of Don's condo. He staggered out the vehicle and made his way through the luxurious building. He did his best to cover the blood as he navigated to his front door. As soon as he entered his condo, he headed straight to the bathroom to examine the small wound on his neck. Warm water was running out the faucet, soaking into a washcloth and being used to wipe away the blood from his neck. He was still in shock about everything that happened. The sun began rising, and for Don, it was more than just a symbol.

"Are you ok?" a soft voice asked.

Don immediately turned around to get a look at the uninvited guest. "What the fuck are you doing here?"

"I came here to talk."

"There's nothing to talk about. You're a fuckin lair, and a fuckin' pig."

"Let me explain."

"How could you possibly explain this? What were you trying to do? Are you the reason I got arrested in the first place?" Don walked up to Ayanna, looking into her watery eyes. The mascara that ran down her face hadn't been wiped off.

"I didn't want to tell you I was on the force because you wouldn't have wanted me. Things wouldn't have gotten to where they were with us if you knew I was a detective. You know I had nothing to do with you getting arrested."

"I don't know shit. All I know is that you spent most of your time lying to me. So tell me what's next? Should I expect the cops to kick in my door with a warrant?"

"Why would they be kicking in your door? Are you hiding something?"

"Hell no, but who knows what the fuck you got up your sleeve. You almost got me killed tonight," Don said, pointing to the puncture wound on his neck.

"Who did this to you?" Ayanna asked, attempting to wipe away the blood that was running down Don's neck.

He smacked her hand away and turned to pick up the washcloth again. Ayanna reached down and grabbed the washcloth from Don's hand. She gently dabbed the wound, causing him to flinch. Don looked in the mirror at Ayanna. There was something genuine in her eyes. The way she looked back at him made his heart sink into his stomach. He wasn't about to tell her how grateful he was that she saved their lives in the club. "Tell me the truth. What are you after?"

"When it comes to you, I'm not after anything."

"What about when it comes to everyone else?"

"Don, I know all about the Street Kings and what y'all do. Just leave the crew."

"What do we do? I do nothing but buy and sell property. You know exactly what I do."

"That's why you need to leave the crew. Look at last night. Some guys showed up to kill you and your cousin, on your birthday, and you're acting like that is something normal. Why do you want that type of life?"

"I never said I wanted that type of life. I don't even know who those guys were."

"That's exactly my point. There are so many people out here that are going to come after you, and you don't even know who they are. Your cousin and his crew are putting your life in danger. I wouldn't be surprised if they did that to your neck."

"You did this shit to my neck," Don barked while gripping Ayanna up by her shoulders. No one had ever made Don this mad before. He couldn't even look at Ayanna without thinking about her whipping out the gun and badge from her purse. "You just put a fuckin' target on my back."

"I didn't mean to. I swear. Things just got out of control."

A part of Don wanted to send the back of his hand across Ayanna's face. No excuse she made would justify her actions. Everything was now coming full circle; the day they met, catching her snooping around the condo, and all the questions that were asked. Don was pissed at Ayanna, but even more so with himself. He should have known. The signs were all there, but he was blinded by love. Don released Ayanna from his death grip. Assaulting an officer wouldn't have been the best idea in the world, especially since he feared returning to prison. "You need to tell me everything," Don ordered after regaining his composure.

"What do you mean by everything?" Ayanna asked. Tears poured from her eyes as she saw the pain she had caused Don.

"I need to know why you chose me. What were you trying to do?"

Ayanna shook her head, and then wiped her eyes with her forearm. Her emotions were getting the best of her. She hadn't imagined facing Don would be this difficult. Ayanna had worked several of undercover investigations in the past and never became emotionally attached to any of the suspects. She made the arrests without regrets or remorse. Families were broken apart and lives were changed forever, but that didn't matter as long as she got her suspect. Ayanna wasn't even close to arresting the Street Kings and was so caught up.

"What were you trying to do? What were you after?"

Ayanna sniffled. "I wanted to bring down your organization. All of you." She flinched as a closed fist came flying toward her. Just missing her face by inches, Don punched a hole in the wall. "You are poisoning people with these drugs you are pumping out on the streets," she yelled out.

Don looked away. He wasn't proud of how the organization obtained their income, but he knew their vision was bigger than drug distribution. In a few more years, their real estate investments would allow them to retire from the drug game. This was Don's plan for the group. No more drugs, no more killing, and no more time spent in jail. Just living life on the up and up.

"See, you have nothing to say. You know you are better than all of that, Don."

"That's not us."

"Yes, it is. It has always been since the organization started. So many people have died going up against your organization."

"My organization? My organization specializes in the purchasing of residential and commercial buildings. I have no idea what you are talking about with these killings and drugs," Don responded, feeling like he was being interrogated.

"Don't play Don. I know about the killings. I know about the cards. Don't play dumb with me."

"Where are you getting this shit from? If we killed anyone, then why aren't we in jail? Why haven't you locked me up yet?"

"It's not you, baby. It's —"

"Don't call me baby. You don't even think about callin' me that shit ever again."

"There are murderers in your organization, Don. You know it. Your uncle was a murderer too."

"You better shut the fuck up. You don't know my fuckin' uncle!" Don barked, getting in Ayanna's face.

"I was the first officer on scene at your uncle's crime scene."

Don stepped back and processed the statement. For years, they received no information into his uncle's unsolved murder. The streets had no answers, the police had no answers, and the family was left wondering what really happened to Corey King.

"What do you mean you were the first on scene?"

"I was brand new, and I was the first to pull up to the car fire. "

"So you know who killed my uncle?"

"No. I pulled up, and there was no one around the vehicle. I was so new that I didn't know what to do, but I do know things didn't seem right. Other cops handled the investigation, and I got shut out."

"Do you think the cops killed my uncle?"

"I don't know. Maybe they knew the killer."

Don couldn't believe what he was hearing. The possibility of the police being behind the murder of his uncle was shocking, but not unbelievable. Atlanta Police had a beef with the Street Kings from the moment the organization was formed. In the past, officers not only looked at the organization as drug dealers, but they were also an organization that infiltrated their department. Officers became corrupt and were on Corey King's payroll, which offended officers that took the oath seriously.

"I need to find out what happened to my uncle," Don pleaded.

"How are you going to do that?"

"Is there anything you can do?"

"I don't know. The case is so old."

"I need you to get me in contact with the detective that investigated the case?"

Ayanna thought about the request. Knowing the department, it would be a difficult task. "Since it was so long ago, how do we know if that detective is still on the job?"

"I don't care where they are. I just need a name. I will find them—"

"—And do what?" Ayanna asked skeptically.

"I need answers. I'm not going to do anything else."

"I don't believe you, Don."

"You're the last fuckin' person that needs to be casting judgment when it comes to believing what someone says."

"Well, I will get the answers you need."

"I want them right now," Don said. He walked to the front door and opened it.

"Are you serious right now?"

"Dead serious. Find out who killed my uncle."

# Chapter 26

"You can't be serious!" Sergeant Packard barked. "How many more cases are we going to get? Bodies are dropping every damn day." He pulled up on the 600 block of Dalvigney Street, greeted by a mob of police officers and an even larger crowd of onlookers. He took a sip of his iced coffee before stepping out the Ford Taurus. He ducked under the police tape and made his way toward the front entrance of The Cut. Several white sheets were placed on the sidewalk in front of the apartment building. Sergeant Packard didn't need to lift the sheets to know what was under each one. *Somebody lit this place up*, he thought as he saw the barrage of shell casings that covered the ground and surrounded the sheet-covered bodies.

"Good morning Joe," Lieutenant Anderson welcomed.

"It's morning, but I don't know if I would say it's a good one. What the hell happened here?"

"What, out here? This ain't nothing compared to the courtyard."

Sergeant Packard looked around again and easily counted six bodies on the sidewalk. He walked up the steps to the courtyard and saw seven white sheets surrounding a thick tree. He noticed numerous bloody chains hanging from the tree limbs. Although police officers were securing the lower level of the apartment building, many of the residents flooded the balconies on the remaining floors. Some were yelling at the officers below and others had their phones out, recording the activity. Several residents were representing their affiliation with the D-Block gang, by sporting the familiar black bandana.

There wasn't much Sergeant Packard hadn't seen during his fifteen years in the homicide unit and twelve years on the streets prior, but this crime scene took the cake. He walked over to the tree, stepping over the sheets. His curiosity focused on the bloody chains because this would be a first for him. He investigated a hanging during his first year as a homicide detective, but it was race related and a group of racists was responsible for that murder. This was much different. The chains couldn't possibly be the instrument of the crime. *Rope would have been much easier to use for strangulation, so why use chains?*

CL LOWRY

"Bizarre, huh?" Lieutenant Anderson asked, standing behind Sergeant Packard.

"Were the chains used in the murders?"

"Nope. It seems like they were just used to string up the bodies."

Sergeant Packard bent down and peeked under one of the sheets. He cringed when he saw Yvette's naked, mutilated body. Bruises covered her face, her throat had been slashed, and her hands and feet were missing. The cut marks on her wrists and ankles suggested a machine was used to make the precise amputations. "What the hell is this? This looks like a mob hit."

"You don't even know the half of it. Each of them is like that. Missing their hands and feet with their throats cut. There are two kids here too."

"Kids?"

"Yup. A five-year-old and seven-year-old."

Sergeant Packard's stomach twisted up when he heard the ages. The youngest homicide victim he dealt with was a ten-year-old that was struck by a stray bullet in Bankhead. Even dealing with that was hard, but he couldn't imagine the animals that would cut the hands and feet off a child. "Who the fuck did this?"

"These were found shoved in the mouths of each of the victims."

Sergeant Packard grabbed the evidence bags from the Lieutenant. *The Jack of Hearts. The Ace of Spades. The fuckin' Street Kings.* Each of the cards was riddled with blood. He couldn't believe that people who had just beaten a federal case would be involved in such a gruesome crime. "What is the motive here?"

"Well, there is a little irony in this one. Remember the kid that went to the hospital, from your club shooting?"

"Yeah, what about him?"

"The sheet you lifted up was his little sister. Next to her, you have his mother, and the others are his grandmother, uncle, kids, and the mother of his kids. These hits were very personal."

"He is the head of the D-Block gang. I wonder if they have a beef with anyone. This could be the result of a street war."

"I don't know, Joe. If it were just a street war, they would just kill them. Cutting off body parts and hanging the bodies out on display is some cartel shit."

"Are there any witnesses?"

Lieutenant Anderson chuckled. "Do you think anyone wants to step forward in this case? We have a better chance asking the deceased what happened, rather than any of these people out here."

Sergeant Packard looked around the apartment complex once more, seeing if anyone looked the least bit concerned with helping solve the murders. Most of the residents seemed angry and were still yelling down toward them. *Finding a cooperative witness is going to be like finding a needle in a haystack.*

# Chapter 27

Cash woke up to the sound of his phone ringing. Everything that took place in the days prior seemed like a long nightmare, and he was hoping none of it was true. Once he saw Reana sleeping next to him and the dress she wore to the club laid out on the floor, he knew it was all real. He reached toward the nightstand, where he usually kept the phone but didn't feel it. The ringing stopped, and Cash rolled back over, figuring the caller would leave a message. Suddenly the phone began ringing again. *What the fuck*? He thought as he sat up and looked around the room. He located the ringing coming from his pants, which were next to Reana's dress. Cash pulled his phone out the pants pocket and checked to see who was blowing him up.

"Sup Nicolás?" Cash answered.

"Cristóbal, have you heard anything yet?"

"No, not yet. It has been a lot going on in the streets, and everything has been hush-hush."

"¡Dios mío! I need to find my boys. We have shipments that need to be delivered."

"We can come to pick up our shipment if you want. I know we dealt with your sons in the past but what the hell happened while I was locked away?"

"I don't know. One day I was talking to my boys, and the next minute they weren't returning my phone calls. Their phones don't even ring anymore, Cristóbal. We both know what that means."

"Are you sure they didn't get locked up or something?"

"If they did, one of them would have called me. I have resources that have checked arrest records around the country, and nothing comes up regarding my boys. My wife and Maria are devastated. I need answers."

"I'm trying to get you answers Nicolás, but no one has heard anything."

"WELL, TRY HARDER!" Nicolás roared. The frustration in his voice was evident. The small talk at the beginning of their conversation was eating him alive. Nicolás would rather have his enemies make it known that there was animosity. He would respect that more than the hidden agendas and dishonesty.

"Listen, man. You need to calm down. I know this is a hard time for you and your family, but there is nothing I can do unless I have more information."

Nicolás took a deep breath and hung his head low. The normally composed drug lord was allowing his emotions to get the best of him. He never wanted Cash to see the hand he was playing because he still needed to know the truth of what happened to his sons. He had an empire to pass down, and they were the heirs to the throne. He hadn't envisioned this life for Maria. The last thing he wanted was his daughter caught up in the streets. She was his precious gem, and there was no way he would allow anyone to treat her any other type of way.

"Hello?" Cash asked, wondering why it suddenly got silent.

"En boca cerrada no entran moscas," Nicolás muttered to himself.

He used his handkerchief to wipe his eyes before placing it on the table next to the rifle that was sitting in front of him. A gift from his sons, the solid gold AK-47 was more than just a powerful weapon. It was a symbol of their family. He looked at their bond as rare, strong, and desirable. Nothing could break that bond, but Nicolás never expected someone to take it away.

"Nicolás are you there?"

"Can I ask you something Cristóbal?"

"Yeah, you can."

"If you were me what would you do?"

Cash didn't feel like playing Nicolás' game. Deep down he wanted to tell him the truth about what happened to his sons and why it had to happen. "I know exactly what you should do. You should schedule a time and place for my people to pick up the shipment. Get back to business and let me worry about your sons."

"Let you worry about them? Honestly, you don't seem too worried."

"I am, but I still have mouths feed. If you want the streets to give you something, then you have to give them something. You know how this works."

"You're right Cristóbal. I will send you a time and location, and you can have your men pick up the shipment. I will handle the business until I find my sons." Nicolás immediately hung up the phone and placed it on the table. He picked up the AK-47 and aimed it straight. Looking through the sights, he aimed at a newspaper article from the Street Kings' arrest.

"You know they killed your sons, right?"

Nicolás' aim slowly went from the newspaper article to the young man that sitting across from him at the table. After the deals at The Cut apartments, Nicolás rode around the streets of Atlanta trying to find his sons. He stumbled upon the young man who was on the streets. The young man seemed broken, but Nicolás didn't mind because he needed an ear in the streets. Cash didn't appear to be doing his job, so Nicolás was willing to give someone else the opportunity to step up. After receiving a significant amount of details regarding the relationship between the Colombians and The Street Kings, the young man needed very little time to come up with his conclusion. Nicolás was locked on to the young man's chest with the AK-47. Despite wearing a white tank top, a fresh tattoo could be seen covering his chest and shoulder. The detailed angels and halos drawn over four names made the memorial peace stand out. "How are you so sure that my sons are dead?"

"The same way I'm sure that my sister and nephews are dead. I know how the Street Kings operate. They run the streets and could have info on your boys in minutes. They aren't telling you anything because it's gon' come back to them."

"What proof do you have?"

"Proof? I don't have any proof, but that doesn't mean you can't find some. Check everything your sons had. Their homes, social media pages, phone records and whatever else you can get your hands on. You do that, and I guarantee you it will lead you back to the Street Kings."

"So what is your beef with the Street Kings? Why are you so adamant they had something to do with the disappearance of my sons?"

"The Street Kings did so much for me. They fed me, put money in my pockets, and allowed me to learn everything about the game. I considered them family—"

Nicolás inserted a magazine into the rifle and chambered a round. "El hijo de puta."

"No, no, no. They were family, but they aren't anymore. Just like you, I'm missing the people that were closest to me, and I won't stop until everyone in that crew is underground. I can build an army, but I need resources. If you are willing to help me, I am willing to eliminate your enemy. I will destroy the Street Kings and leave that throne drenched in blood."

Nicolás couldn't help but smile. This was music to his ears.

"What did you say your name was again, boy?"

"Deuce, the name's Deuce."

# Chapter 28

Staring out the front passenger window of the Ford Focus, looking just past the other police cars in the parking lot, Detective Knowles listened in on Ayanna's conversation. He would kill to hear who was on the other end but based on Ayanna's strange demeanor, he knew it had something to do with the Street Kings. He looked at his watch for the fifth time in the past hour as minutes began ticking away. Agitation and hunger were getting the best of him. *Why the hell are we still sitting here*, he thought as he waited for Ayanna to finish her conversation.

"Please give me a chance to prove myself to you. My feelings are real," Ayanna said, hoping Don didn't hang up the phone on her. After being up all night, she had time to think about everything that occurred. Things needed to be prioritized in her life because there was no way she would be able to hold on to her career and Don. The investigation was supposed to be simple, and she was never supposed to catch feelings for a man she was trying to put behind bars. Even if a pile of solid evidence against the Street Kings suddenly appeared on her desk, her heart would no longer let her pursue any of them. Betraying Don would not be worth throwing away true love.

Detective Knowles pushed his face up in repugnance. In all the years he has worked with Ayanna, he had never seen her as vulnerable as she was now. She was a woman that laughed in the face of adversity and took on the hardest challenges that many people wouldn't even consider taking on. Now he sat in a car next to a woman who was begging a man to give her a second chance. A man, Detective Knowles didn't even think was on her level. *I can't believe this scumbag has her wrapped around his finger. She deserves a real man.* He couldn't take it any longer. He swung open the car door and made a hasty exit.

"Hey, let me call you right back," Ayanna told Don after noticing her partner's impulsive reaction. She slowly drove beside her partner as he walked up the quickly street. "Cliff, what are you doing?"

"Getting the hell away from you!" he barked.

Ayanna was taken aback by his response. She had seen her partner pissed off plenty of times when they made arrests, but this was the first time he gave her attitude. "Why? What did I do?"

"What did you do? The same shit you always do."

"What's that supposed to mean?" Ayanna asked as she slammed the car in park and got out.

"I'm not going there with you Ayanna."

"Oh yes, you are. You can't just snap on me and not tell me why you're acting like this."

"Does it even matter to you?"

"Yes, it does."

"I have been by your side from the moment I saw you. Each and every time you get into some bullshit, I'm there to clean it up. I have been doing this for years. Do you appreciate it? No. You walk around here like I'm not shit to you. Then you go and start this dumb ass investigation and fall for one of those fuckin' criminals."

"You don't know what you're talking about." Ayanna couldn't even keep a straight face when she made the statement.

"I know you all too well. I see the look on your face when you're on the phone with him. You took this investigation on by yourself and have yet to report back with anything, not to mention you shot a guy in a crowded club."

"I had no other choice. He had a gun pointed in my direction."

"Pointed in your direction or your new boyfriend's direction?"

Ayanna didn't say a word. She was still confused as to why they were having that particular conversation.

She was a single woman and answered to no man but her father....and Don.

"So which one is it?"

"Huh?"

"Which one of those thugs are you dating? Is it Chris King? Are you going after the head of the organization?"

Silence.

"Or maybe it's Don King. How about Ace Newton? The Ace of Spades. The fuckin' killer. Are you serious, Ayanna? These are the people you want to associate with?"

Ayanna rolled her eyes and walked back to the car. *I don't have to take this shit*, she thought as she tried not to get emotional. Her partner had a point. A month ago, she wouldn't dare associate herself with any type of criminal and because of the investigation she found herself in bed with a leader of one of the most dangerous criminal organizations in Atlanta.

"So you just gon' walk away from me? I would never walk away from you," he shouted, grabbing Ayanna by the wrist and turning her around. "I love you, and I want to be with you."

Those words caught Ayanna off guard. She would have never expected them to come out of her partner's mouth. They worked together for years, and he never made a pass at her. Even if she was slightly attracted to him, he wasn't half the man Don was. No one could compare to her king. Ayanna was too busy thinking about Don that she didn't even notice Detective Knowles had grabbed her by the waist. She snapped out her thoughts just in time to see him leaning in for a kiss.

"What the fuck are you doing?" she yelled out, pushing him away from her. They both didn't realize they were still near police headquarters. All eyes were on them as their coworkers tried to figure out what was going on.

"You really gon' do that to me in front of everybody?" Detective Knowles asked angrily. He knew the embarrassment he just experienced would be the number one topic on the rumor mill around the department.

"Do what to you? Don't you ever try to kiss me! Whatever feelings you have are not mutual, Cliff."

His heart shattered into pieces. Ayanna made her choice, and it would be a choice he would make her regret. He looked around as his peers pointed and laughed. His sadness quickly turned to anger and rage. "You are finished. I'm going to take down the Street Kings and you right along with them." Detective Knowles stormed off, leaving Ayanna wondering what he meant by the threats.

# Chapter 29

Ramir inhaled the kush and passed the blunt Nate. They were parked outside Grady Memorial Hospital waiting for Apryl, who was a nurse at the hospital but also another chick on Ramir's roster. The interior of the black Dodge Durango filled up with smoke from the burning herb, and the two men checked the clock.

"Damn bro, where she at?" Nate asked. He was getting impatient.

"I don't know man. She should be coming out soon."

"Well, you know we gotta' go pick up this shipment from the Colombians. Cash is gon' kill us if we don't pick up this work."

"Don't worry about it. Ace is meeting us over there, so he can hold things down for us if we are late."

"Oh shit, look," Nate said, pointing to the thick nurse that was walking toward the SUV. Her scrubs hugged her hips and round ass. Even at the hospital, Apryl turned heads. Her chocolate skin glistened as the Durango's headlights shined on her. She entered the Durango, sliding in the front passenger seat. Ramir greeted her with a kiss on the cheek. "What's up gorgeous?" he asked softly.

"Don't be trying to sweet talk me Mir. What you need?"

"Damn Apryl, it's strictly business huh?" Nate chimed in. He took a puff of the blunt and then offered it to Apryl.

She grabbed the blunt and sealed her full lips around it. She took a deep breath, inhaling the smoke. Both Ramir and Nate were staring at her, mesmerized at how she made smoking look sexy. If Nate weren't in the vehicle, Ramir would surely try to get into Apryl's pants. After a few more puffs, she blew the smoke in Ramir's face. "So why were you blowing my phone up about the dude that got shot the other night?"

"Cuz I wanted to know if that bitch was still alive."

Apryl rolled her eyes. She had a gut feeling that this visit from Ramir was going to lead to her doing something illegal, but she wasn't prepared for what he was about to ask her to do. "Please don't tell me you shot him."

Ramir bust out laughing and Nate followed suit. "Now you know if I shot him, he would be in the morgue, not the hospital."

"Fuckin' right," Nate added, before slapping hands with Ramir.

"But seriously, I need him to disappear," Ramir told Apryl.

"What? There are two cops up there guarding him. What the hell can I do?"

Ramir smirked and opened the center console. He handed Apryl a syringe filled with a tan, liquid substance. She examined the mysterious liquid, wondering what it was. "This can't be heroin because this amount will kill him instantly."

"Don't worry about what it is. It's better that you don't know anyway." He reached back into the center console and pulled out a wad of cash. Apryl's eyes widened once she spotted the cash. It had to be about six months of her salary rolled up in a rubber band. "Let me know when it's done." Apryl leaned in and kissed Ramir on the lips before exiting the Durango and making her way back into the hospital. "Ok come on. Let's got meet these motherfuckin' Colombians," Ramir said to Nate. They two pulled off, leaving Apryl behind to handle their problem.

You couldn't tell what was worse, Apryl's horrible attempt to hide the syringe and cash or the stupid smirk on her face. She was already spending the cash in her head. Furniture, clothes, shoes, and purses were just a few things on her list of purchases to be made once she got off work. The contents of the needle were meant to take a life and she knew it, but her personal agenda was more important than what her conscience was telling her. Her goal was to be Ramir's main chick, and she would do anything for him. Performing this task for him would guarantee her a top spot in his life, or so she thought.

It is ironic that the hospital is the same place they met years ago when he came in as a patient with a gunshot wound to his right shoulder. The moment Apryl saw him she was immediately attracted to him. Ramir was attracted to Apryl too, but when he spotted her and found out she was a nurse, he had to make it happen. Having someone on the inside of one of Atlanta's most popular trauma hospitals was important. If they need a member of their crew patched up without the cops being involved, all they had to do was call Apryl. However, in this case, it's the total opposite. They needed a member of an opposing crew eliminated.

Apryl hopped off the elevator and worked her way down the hallway. She spotted the officers outside the room and as usual, all eyes were on her. They were shooting their shot earlier in the night, with flirtatious comments as she walked by. This was the perfect opportunity to shoot her shot back. "Did you guys miss me?" she asked as she approached the room.

"You know we did," one of the officers said. His eyes focused on her body the entire time.

"Well, I have to check on our little friend in here."

"Go ahead. He's a dirtball anyway, no one cares what happens to him," the other officer said as he opened the door to let Apryl inside the room. She remembered their protocol is to escort the medical staff and standby in the room with them.

"I need you to do me a favor."

"What kind of favor?" he asked, licking his lips.

"It's been a long day, and I need to unwind when I get off. I would like some company when I get off, so can you go out there with your partner and figure out which one of you will be going home with me later."

The officer was speechless, and any words that attempted to escape his mouth weren't understandable. Apryl laughed as she watched him fumble with the doorknob as he let. *What an idiot*, she thought. They didn't even realize she could hear them through the door as they giggled like schoolchildren. Time wasn't on her side, so Apryl had to act fast. She looked at the wounded man as he rested in the bed. His right wrist handcuffed to the bed's side rail. The heart monitor beeped steadily. Apryl grabbed his arm and removed the syringe from her pocket. She found a vein directly above the IV insert and jabbed the needle into the vein, shooting the tan liquid into his body. Apryl thought for sure he would begin convulsing, but he didn't. Antonio just continued resting, not knowing a slow-acting poison had just been injected into his bloodstream. The Street Kings were smart. The last thing they needed was an immediate reaction from the body, which would have tipped off the officers and gotten Apryl caught. Instead, Antonio's body will try to fight off the concoction until it is too weak to keep up the battle. This five-hour ordeal will leave all of his organs shut down and give Apryl enough time to be home and in bed, before anyone suspected any foul play. She placed the cap back on the syringe, tucked it in her pocket, and left the room.

"So did we come up with a choice yet?" she asked the officers, wondering which one of them would be hers.

"Me, I'm all yours," one of the officers said, displaying his confidence.

Apryl looked at the officer who had stepped forward and then glanced back at his partner who had fumbled on the doorknob earlier. He was still acting timid and made no eye contact with her. "I'll see you later tonight, handsome," Apryl told the officer standing in the back. He was shocked at her response. After getting his phone number, Apryl walked away knowing she made the right choice. *I have my alibi for tonight*, she thought. Once the poison finished working its way through Antonio's body, she would be in the company of the officer, and no one would ever consider her a suspect in his murder.

# Chapter 30

Ayanna slammed her fingers on the keyboard as she typed quickly. She wanted to run Corey King through the police department's in-house system to get the details of his murder. No matter how many times she typed the name in the search bar, a *NO RECORD FOUND* message is all she got back. *This is impossible.* There had to be a record of the case. She sat back in her chair for a while, wondering how this was even possible. Ayanna leaned forward and went back to work on the keyboard. She entered S-T-R-E-E-T-K-I-N-G-S and a list of results immediately came back. She scanned through the list, taking a mental note of the type of cases that were displayed on the screen.

*DRUG DISTRIBUTION...SUSPECT: CHRISTOPHER KING*

*HOMICIDE...SUSPECT: ACE NEWTON*

*DRUG DISTRIBUTION...SUSPECT:
CHRISTOPHER KING
DRUG DISTRIBUTION...SUSPECT: DONOVAN
KING
DRUG DISTRIBUTION...SUSPECT: ACE
NEWTON
HOMICIDE...SUSPECT: ACE NEWTON
HOMICIDE...SUSPECT: ACE NEWTON*

"Hey Cliff, do you know why a case wouldn't be showing up on our system?"

"What case?" Detective Knowles asked.

"The Corey King murder."

Detective Knowles pushed his face up and stood up from his desk. "You can't be serious. You are still on this thing?"

"No, it's not like that. I'm done with the investigation, but I need to find some things out."

"What things?"

"I need to know if there were any suspects in the case."

"Why? What does that have to do with you?" he asked. He paused for a second, looking at the obvious expression on Ayanna's face. "Oh, I get it. This isn't for you, is it?"

"It is for me," she quickly shot back.

"No, it's not. It is probably for your little boyfriend." Jealousy was written all over his face. "Come on; I'll show you where to find what you're looking for."

Ayanna followed her partner to the lower level of the building. He opened the door and headed down the short hallway. "What is down here?" she asked while exploring a part of the building she never knew existed.

"The records vault is down here. Any job that is older than ten years is kept down here. You can find a parking ticket from the 1990s if you looked hard enough."

"But why would a homicide case be here instead of at their building?"

"The original case file is over at the homicide unit, but a copy of it should be in here as well. Supervisors are the only ones with permission to the vault, but I'll see if the officer guarding the vault will give us a pass."

"Well, what if they don't let us in the vault?"

"Then we will have to distract the guard so that you can get into the vault."

"I think that plan is better anyway. I kind of want to keep this whole thing quiet."

"Ok. Well, you wait here and I'll distract the officer who is guarding the vault."

Ayanna nodded her head and backed up behind a wall. She watched as her partner entered the room. Seconds felt like minutes and minutes felt like hours as she waited patiently in the hallway. She could hear chatter coming from the room, but it was difficult to make out what was being said. Voices were also coming from the far end of the hallway as well. Not trying to be spotted by other officers passing through, Ayanna continued hugging the wall. Moments later, Detective Knowles came strutting out the room alongside side a female officer. The older officer was conversing with the detective as he led her toward the stairs.

Ayanna wasted no time slipping into the room. She immediately bypassed rows of shelves that were stocked with hundreds of accordion files. Each file was a different police incident, and each shelf represented a different month in a different year. Ayanna wished she had time to check out some of the files for amusement purposes, but she was on a specific mission. Ayanna continued moving until she reached the large, protected door. There was a keypad on the large door. Ayanna was concerned about the keypad because clearly, she didn't have the code. She turned back, ensuring no one had entered the room. Ayanna grabbed the door handle, and to her surprise, it opened. Swinging open the vault door, she entered the insulated room that was filled with shelves. The shelves contained cardboard boxes that were filled with documentation and copies of evidence from some of the biggest crimes in the city. Ayanna immediately checked each shelf, noticing they were labeled by years. Once she located 2008, she worked her way down the aisle to locate the box she was looking for.

Although she was in the 2008 section, that didn't make it easier to find what she was looking for. Surprisingly, there were several case files on the shelf for that particular year. Ayanna began diving into each box, looking for any documents that will identify her case. She flipped through all types of cases; extortion, bank robbery, arson, human trafficking and more. Time was ticking, and sweat was dripping down Ayanna's face. She grabbed the next box and opened it up. *HOMICIDE...UNSOLVED...KING, COREY.* Ayanna wanted to jump for joy when she found the file. The file seemed to be thinner than what she expected. There were investigation reports and photographs from the scene, but there no witness statements.

Seeing the photographs of the scene brought back so many memories for Ayanna. The flames, the charred car, feeling like she could have done more, and the suspicion of the other officers that arrived as soon as she came over the radio with her transmission. All she vaguely remembered was the investigators pushing her to the side and not involving her in the actual investigation. She never got the name of the investigator, but she was about to find out. Ayanna thumbed through the paperwork until she got her hands on the actual investigation report, which she pulled out to see who it was prepared by. Her heart sunk into her stomach and her legs got weak. *Prepared by...DETECTIVE JOSEPH PACKARD.*

"Hey, what are you doing," a voice said from inside the room.

Ayanna looked back and saw Captain Therian advancing toward her. He had a team of supervisors and the guarding officer with him. She was stuck like a deer in headlights. There were no exits, no escaping the encounter.

"What are you doing in here?" Captain Therian asked again.

"I was just chec—checking a cold case," she hesitantly replied.

"With whose permission?"

Ayanna had no answer. She didn't want to throw her partner under the bus because he was doing her a favor. She slowly closed the box and stepped forward, out the vault. The supervisors and administrators all looked at Ayanna, who knew she had messed up. She looked at each of the faces in the small group and was in disbelief when she saw her partner standing amongst the administrators. *He set me up*, she thought as she briefly locked eyes with him.

"You need to hand me your badge," Captain Therian ordered. "You are suspended until further notice."

She had already had her phone and gun taken due to the club shooting investigation, and now her badge was gone. There was no way she would be able to get the answers Don wanted. She needed to get back into that vault.

# Chapter 31

"Damn bro, this ride is long as shit," Nate said, after looking at his watch and realizing they had been on the road for two hours.

"Yo shut the fuck up. You ain't doing shit but sitting over there playing on your phone. I'm the one who's driving, and I knocked forty-five minutes off the time. We should be there soon," Ramir replied. He averaged a hundred miles per hour in the Durango on the way down but knew he wouldn't be able to do that type of speed on the way back. He was proud of himself for making it down on time to meet Ace, and happy Apryl sent him the text message confirming Antonio will no longer be a problem to them. With Antonio and Los out of the picture, the D-Block gang's territory is up for grabs. Ramir wanted that territory and was ready to take it over. Obtaining the territory would mean more money in his pockets and independence within the organization. Although Ramir was the head of the organization when everyone was arrested, he wanted to prove he was more than just a killer.

Ramir pulled up to the Port of Savannah and entered the Garden City Terminal, where he pulled behind Ace's black Lincoln Navigator. The headlights lit up Ace, who was sitting in the bed of the truck, smoking a cigar.

"I thought you were providing security for the pick-up," Ramir said after exiting the Durango.

Ace chuckled but didn't say a word. He exhaled the cigar smoke and pointed toward Ramir's chest as he approached. Ramir looked down and discovered three red lasers pointed at his chest. He looked back at Nate and noticed two lasers dancing around Nate's forehead. He quickly looked up and around the facility. Just as he thought, there was no sign of the gunmen who were aiming.

"Damn, that's crazy," Ramir muttered, admiring the stealthy presence of the gunmen.

The headlights of a tractor-trailer illuminated the three men when it pulled up. Three dark-colored SUVs followed behind the trailer and once it stopped behind Ramir's Durango, the occupants of each SUV quickly exited. Ace watched as the Colombian men stepped out the SUVs and gripped the assault rifles that were slung around their bodies. Ace knew they didn't come with enough firepower to match an assault from the

Colombians, even with the snipers they strategically placed around the terminal. Two of the Colombians opened the rear door of the last SUV. Ace did his best to peek past the frontline henchmen, expecting to get his eyes on Nicolás Muñoz exiting the vehicle. Ace tossed his cigar, which was a signal to his gunman to focus their attention on the head of the Muñoz Cartel. If something were to go wrong with the transaction, Ace planned to cripple the organization by taking out Nicolás.

Ace, Ramir, and Nate stepped forward. Despite knowing they had sniper coverage, Ramir and Nate pulled out handguns from their waistbands. With an extended clip, Ramir was prepared to take out at least six of his opponents. The Colombians tightened the wall as the occupant of the rear SUV began exiting. Ace couldn't get a good view but was sure there would probably be a small meeting between him and Nicolás. This would be the Cartel boss' first appearance at a shipment, and Ace knew there would be questions that needed to be answered. As both sides came face to face, there were a ton of dirty looks and mumbling. The animosity between both sides was obvious.

"Nice to see you gentlemen made it here safely," a voice said. The Colombians parted like the Red Sea, exposing the speaker.

"So what do we owe for this surprise," Ace said when he saw Maria Muñoz emerge from the rear of the group.

"Hey Ace, long time no see," she said. Maria and Ace greeted each other with a hug and a kiss on the cheek. The two hadn't seen each other since one of her brother's threw a big birthday bash, a few years prior. Maria was so beautiful. She was average height, with high cheek bones, hazel eyes, black hair that was down to her lower back, and a slim figure. Most men were terrified of Maria because of her family's reputation. It was rumored that one of her ex-boyfriends cheated on her and was decapitated and his head was never located.

Along with the beauty, she had brains as well. Maria was the baby in the family and was always trying to prove herself. Her father did his best to keep her out the drug game, but she made sure she inserted herself in it.

"What are you doing here?" Ace asked while trying not to focus on her cleavage.

"I'm here to make a delivery and to see an old friend."

"Where's ya pops?"

"He—uh—had to go back to Colombia to handle some business."

"Is everything ok?"

"Yeah, of course. It's just something small."

"Well, I guess this is for you." Ace had a duffle bag stuffed with money in his hand. He extended the bag toward Maria, and one of the men by her side grabbed it. He zipped open the bag and began rifling through the stacks of cash.

"¿Cómo es?" Maria asked her henchman.

"Parece que todo el dinero está aquí, jefe," the man replied.

"Ok old friend, Hector is your driver and he will deliver your shipment once you give him the address." Maria signaled for the driver, and he exited the tractor-trailer and headed toward the three.

"Nate, give the driver the directions to the warehouse. Ramir, put the gun up."

"Ramir?" Maria asked, after hearing the name being said. "You're Ramir?"

"Yeah that's me shawty," the young boss replied.

"I've heard so much about you."

"From who?" Ace asked. He didn't receive an answer from Maria. He wanted to know how his little cousin's name became a topic of conversation to the cartel.

"I'm sure you heard nothing but good things," Ramir said while stepping forward and getting closer to Maria. Two members from the cartel stepped forward also, showing their displeasure for Ramir's flirtatious mannerism. "Damn, y'all hype as shit. I'm not gon' hurt the little princess."

"You better be careful Papi. I'm a queen, and that's how you should treat me."

"Well Queen, I apologize. How can I make it up to you?"

"Ok, ok, can we stick to the program?" Ace butted in. He was not feeling the energy being displayed by Ramir and Maria. The last thing he needed was his cousin in bed with the cartel. That would do nothing but lead to bullet holes and broken hearts. If Ramir hurt Maria, the cartel would be out to hurt Ramir. "The driver has the directions and y'all have your money, so tell Nicolás to hit me up when it's time for the next delivery."

"Come on Ace; there is no need to be strictly business. We are still friends, aren't we?" Maria asked.

"Yeah, we cool but it's time for us to get back to Atlanta."

"Ok, I understand," Maria muttered. She turned to Ramir, who had his eyes locked on her. "I'll be in touch."

Ramir responded with a head nod and smile. He turned and walked back to the Durango. Maria and her men watched their adversaries enter their vehicles. They pulled out the port, followed by the tractor-trailer. Once they were out of sight, the door to one of the SUVs opened. "What was all of that about?"

"It's him. That was Ramir."

"I'm surprised you handled yourself that well."

"Oh father, I don't know why you continue to doubt me. As of now, I am next in line to run the cartel and I will prove to you that I am more than capable of ruling just as well as you."

"So what about the Street Kings?" Nicolás asked.

"For now, we will let the continue making us money."

"What about the Ramir kid?"

"Let me take care of him."

"How are you going to do that?"

"I don't know yet. All I know is that I want his heart."

# Chapter 32

Don laid out two suits on the bed, trying to decide which one to choose from. He was scheduled to look at an office building in downtown Atlanta. The navy blue suit was usually his go to, but the light gray suit seemed to be calling his name. The crisp white shirt and gray, lavender, and purple plaid tie made the decision even harder. In Don's eyes being fashionably professional was one of his best characteristics. His suits were all tailored and fit him perfectly. His phone began ringing, and he headed into the kitchen to answer it.

He looked at the number displayed on the screen. *Who the hell is calling me from a 6-0-9 area code?* "Who 'dis?" Don asked when he answered the phone.

"Don from Atlanta, buon giorno. How are you doing?"

Don didn't know too many Italians, so once he heard the accent, he immediately knew it was Big Al.

"Al, what's going on? How have things been?"

"Things have been good my friend. I heard about your case, and I'm happy for you and your family.

"Thank you. So what do I owe the pleasure of your call today?"

"I just wanted to make sure you still were going to do right by me, for looking out for you while you were in here."

"Of course I am Al. I owe you, and I will be ready to repay my debt when the time comes."

"Well Don, that time is now. I need you in New Jersey as soon as possible."

"How soon are you talking?"

"Today."

"Al, I don't think I can make it there today. You literally aren't giving me any time to pack. Plus, I am about to go look at a property downtown."

"Don, I wasn't asking. If you take a look out your window, you will be a silver Ford Explorer. There are four of my men in the vehicle. Either you will go down to them, or they will be coming up to get you. The choice is yours."

Don walked to the window and sure enough, there was the Explorer. He didn't know what to say or do. Don quickly threw on the gray suit pants and the shirt and headed out the door. He didn't even bother putting on the tie or suit jacket. As soon as the door opened,

Don encountered a brolic man in the hallway outside his room. The man was around 6'3" and had to easily be 230 pounds. He had tanned white skin, black hair, and a full beard. It was no question he was one of Big Al's men. He was dressed in a black suit and the bulge of his gun poked through the front of his suit jacket.

"I'm guessin' you're here for me," Don said sarcastically. The man gripped Don up, threw him against the wall, and patted him down. "I'm not dumb enough to bring a fuckin' gun with me," Don stated. The influx in his voice was a clear indicator that he was a bit irritated by the way he was being treated. The man gave him no response and started walking to the exit. Don locked the door and followed behind. *Fuckin' asshole, if I did have a gun, I'd put a bullet right in the back of his head.* He approached the Ford Explorer, which was holding three other occupants. The occupant in the back seat stepped out and held the door for Don as he entered the vehicle. As soon as all occupants were in the vehicle, Don's phone rang again. The same number was displayed on the screen.

"Hello," he answered.

"I'm glad to see you made the right decision, my friend."

"Are you having me visit you in jail?" Don asked, knowing there was no way the Feds were going to release Big Al.

"Of course not. I can't say much now, but you will meet with my attorney and he will go over everything with you. Since I don't need any more surprises from the Feds, I need you to give your phone and wallet to Lorenzo."

"Are you sure everything is ok?"

"Yes, my friend. Buona giornata!"

"Yeah, you too," Don said, showing off the little bit of Italian he picked during his stay in prison.

Don took his wallet out his pocket and handed it to Lorenzo, along with his phone. The thin Italian man thoroughly checked both items, emptying out the contents of the wallet and physically inspecting the cell phone. Once satisfied, he placed the items in a small plastic bag and tucked it under the seat. Don didn't want to say much because he figured he wouldn't get too many answers from the men in the car. He sat between them and looked straight the entire ride as they drove through Atlanta, heading toward Peachtree City. Don cut his eyes to the right, as soon as Lorenzo pulled out a phone. Out his peripheral, he could see him scroll through the contact list before double tapping on someone's name.

"We are pulling up," Lorenzo said and hung up the phone.

Everything about this situation seemed odd to Don, but as usual, he was analyzing it from a business aspect. It was admirable. Just knowing that Big Al had this type of reach from behind bars was terrifying but impressive. This is the type of power the Street Kings lacked. They struck fear into the streets, but they

shouldn't always have to do so by shedding blood and putting the bodies on display. Don knew if he made the wrong move, there would be a spot in a river where his corpse would be dumped. No one would know what happened to him and the authorities wouldn't have a clue where to begin looking. Although the organization of Big Al's mafia was impressive, Don couldn't help but wonder how Big Al ended up behind bars. The Feds had to have a solid case on him.

The Ford Explorer cruised down Falcon Drive and pulled into the road leading toward Atlanta Regional Airport. The private airfield was known for being the location where rappers, athletes, and celebrities landed their private jets. They pulled up close to an Embraer Legacy 600. The door to the white jet was open, and a portable staircase was already in place to assist the travelers. Two armed guards stood at the staircase, and another was in the doorway of the plane. The Del-Ton Echo AR style rifles the guards toted would surely produce a significant amount of damage to any intruder or threat against the jet. Don didn't know whether to feel protected or nervous.

"Come on. let's go," Lorenzo ordered, stepping out of the vehicle. He, Don and the other occupants of the vehicle ascended the stairs and entered the private jet. The guard in the doorway gave Don a look that could kill. Once he stepped by the guard, Don was taken aback by the layout of the prestigious aircraft. Standing in the aisle, there were luxury recliner chairs on both the left and right side of the aircraft. He had flow first class plenty of times, but that was nothing compared to what he was viewing at the moment. Lorenzo and his men began sitting down and getting comfortable, but Don was still stuck in the aisle. His legs felt like they weighed 1000 pounds. A part of him was in real estate mode, admiring the décor and the other part was in shock.

"Don, it's good to see you again."

Dominic Ricci emerged from a back area. It was good to see a familiar face. The weight was lifted from Don's legs, and he walked over to greet the Big Al's attorney. "Dominic, how have you been?"

"Good and yourself?"

"I am blessed. I want to thank you again for all of your help with my case."

Dominic put his hand on Don's shoulder. "Don't mention it. It was nothing."

"Oh no, it was my freedom."

"Have a seat," Dominic suggested. "Relax, we will be in Jersey in a couple of hours."

Don sank into the leather when he sat down in the chair. The door to the jet was closed, and the pilots began preparing for takeoff. Two flight attendants emerged from the rear of the cabin and immediately caught Don's attention. He could tell they weren't just any flight attendants. Their beautiful faces, long dark hair, and risqué outfits had Big Al written all over. The women brought Don a glass of champagne and an assortment of pastries. As he began partaking, they attended to Lorenzo and his men. The laughter and flirty banter showed everyone knew each other. Don kept his eyes on the women until Dominic was able to regain his attention.

"Looks like you want more than those pastries," Dominic said, laughing at Don.

"No, no, no. I'm good. That seems like nothing but trouble right there."

"Agreed, but trouble isn't always a bad thing."

"Speaking of trouble," Don muttered. "What the hell did I get myself into?"

Lorenzo looked back at Don when the question was asked. Dominic didn't immediately answer. Instead, he grabbed one of the pastries and took a bite, while looking out the window and watching Atlanta get smaller. Ever since he was a young boy, Dominic enjoyed nothing more than flying. When his family took him on vacation, he would always grab the window seat and be glued to the window the entire flight. Being amongst the clouds was an experience that was unexplainable. Once the jet was in the air and on course to New Jersey, Dominic finished his pastry and wiped his mouth with a napkin.

"Big Al needs your expertise."

"With what? Is he looking to buy up property in Jersey?"

"Something like that."

"You handle most of the business acquisitions for the Street Kings right?"

"Yeah, I take our income and invest it into properties, whether it's residential or commercial."

"Where does that income come from?" Don's eyebrows slanted down toward the center of his face and eyes squinted. "It's not like that," Dominic said, noticing the expression on Don's face. "How do you justify the income?"

"What makes you think our income needs to be justified?" Don asked. The hairs on the back of his neck stood up. Once again, he felt like he was being interrogated.

"Ok Don, I'm going to get straight to the point. Big Al didn't just appoint me as your attorney as a favor to you. Being your attorney gave me access to all the evidence the federal prosecutor planned to use against you. This included business transactions, tax filings, and every single bank statement with your name attached to it. Big Al wanted to know how your organization operated and quite frankly, he liked what he saw."

Don didn't know how to respond. He knew there had to be some sort of catch behind Big Al's generosity, but he never expected this. He felt played. He already allowed Ayanna to infiltrate the organization, and if Cash found out the Italians were all in their business too, he would kill Don for being so reckless.

"I'm not doing nothing that y'all haven't been doing for years."

"Yes, you are. You are legitimizing the money you get off the street, and the IRS isn't even batting an eye. How are you doing it?"

"Why do you need to know all that? You are starting to sound like the fuckin' cops."

Dominic chuckled at the accusation. "I eat cops up for breakfast and spit them out. Don't you ever compare me to a pig. There's a reason we are having this conversation in the air, and I'm sure you had to give up your phone."

"That's why y'all took my shit?"

"Yes, it is. We don't trust anyone. The Feds can get to anyone. They got to your friend, Trey Davis, didn't they?

"Yeah, but then he got exactly what he deserved."

"Exactly. We don't have time for those types of mistakes being made in our organization."

"Well, you don't have to worry about that with me. I stay hands off when it comes to how the money is made. I just find ways to make it look good."

"Big Al is sitting on millions of dollars in cash and also millions worth of product. All of it is dirty, and we need you to clean it up."

"Does he own any businesses?"

"Unfortunately he doesn't. Big Al thinks those tactics are old school. There are businesses we run out of, but nothing is in his name."

"Well, that's going to change. Once we get to Jersey, I'll set up an LLC specifically for this operation and then we will need to find some apartments and restaurants in around the state."

"Sounds good. We also have to figure out what to do with this new product he just acquired."

"What kind of product?" Don asked, knowing he stayed away from the drug part of the organization's operations.

Dominic opened a briefcase that contained stacks of money and a small, black cloth bag. Dominic removed the bag and placed it on top of the briefcase. He slid the briefcase over to Don. "There is $250,000 in there for you as an initial payment for your services. There will be another $250,000 waiting for you inside your condo when you get back."

Don grabbed the cloth bag and slid the briefcase back to Dominic.

"Big Al did me a huge favor, and now I'm returning that favor. I don't want his money."

Don opened up the bag, and his eyes lit up. He poured the contents of the bag into the palm of his hand. Dominic smiled when he watched the diamonds pour into Don's hand. They sparkled as light each stone from every angle. Don couldn't believe his eyes. Each diamond was unique in its own way, whether it was size or cut.

"That is half of million dollars' worth of diamonds you are holding in your hand. There is plenty more where that came from, and Big Al needs to find a way to cash them out. It is too much for the black market."

"This is going to be a challenge," Don replied, holding one of the diamonds up to the light.

"Well, I hope you are up for the challenge."

"One thing at a time. Let's get the cash straightened out first and then we can focus on the diamonds. Don poured them back into the bag. He looked down at the floor, ensuring he didn't drop any. The last thing he needed was a $10,000 diamond rolling under the seat. He extended his arm to hand the diamonds back to Dominic.

"Keep them. They are yours."

"Hell no. I can't take these."

"The money was a payment for service, but these are a gift from Big Al."

"This is crazy. I don't know what to say."

"You don't have to say anything at all. The work you put in with us is going to make you a very rich man," Dominic said. He looked over at the window, admiring the perfect view. "You are going from a Street King to the KING OF DIAMONDS."

# Chapter 33

"DAMN PAPI!" Maria screamed as Ramir shoved her head into the mattress and pounded her from the back. She knew once she texted him the address of the hotel she was staying at in Savannah, he would have no problem taking the trip back down. What she didn't expect was him to rock her world in bed. Ramir had Maria pinned, and she was a slave to his will.

"Oh Dios mío, me estás matando."

Ramir didn't speak a lick of Spanish, but Maria's body language was telling him exactly what he wanted to hear. Keeping her pinned to the mattress, he sprawled his legs back and drove his hips forward. Every inch of his rod was now inside her, and she screamed to the top of her lungs. You could hear the sexual screams from down the hallway as Ramir gave Maria strong strokes. Her nails dug into the headboard and her teeth sunk into the pillows, as he repositioned to his knees and increased his stroke speed.

*SMACK!* His hand came crashing down on her right ass cheek.

*SMACK!* His hand came crashing down on her left ass cheek.

*SMACK!* Both hands came crashing down, making contact on both cheeks.

"Oh Dios mío!" she yelled out, enjoying the pleasure and pain. Ramir repeated the actions while he continued stroking. The repeated smacks left abrasions on Maria's ass that would surely be visible for about a week. The young thug admired his work while he continued pounding Maria, doggie-style. In the back of his mind, Ace's warnings were on repeat. *"Stay away from Maria Muñoz. That cartel is trouble."* The warnings didn't stop Ramir from responding to her message about meeting up to discuss business. He wanted to expand his reach and wanted to do it on his terms. Just like Trey, once someone sees himself or herself being bigger than their current role, they move differently.

*This shit feels so fuckin' good*, Ramir thought as he slowly stroked Maria, watching himself go in and out her love box. Every time he reentered, she flinched. His thickness would spread her lips apart and allow him access. Ramir grabbed Maria by the waist and turned her over. As she lay on her back, looking up at him, he admired her beauty. Her hazel eyes drew him right in and before he knew it, he had her legs pinned back, and he was going to work.

"Yes, right there," Maria moaned.

Her nails sunk into his back, locking him in place. She didn't want him changing positions on her because the current position felt like ecstasy. Ramir grabbed her ankles and pushed them down further until they almost touched her head. Then it was back to the planking position and deep strokes. Ramir plunged inside her repeatedly. His scrotum smacked against her asshole during each thrust, causing her to feel a new sensation. She was having some of the best sex of her life. Maria's eyes rolled into the back of her head as she reached her climax. Ramir felt her tighten up and get wetter. He smiled while looking down at her, knowing his mission was accomplished. She grabbed the back of his head and pulled him closer to her. Their lips touched, causing her body to shake. As they kissed, the sensational feeling of being inside of Maria suddenly increased. Ramir's legs began shaking. He tried to keep his momentum, but it would seem to be impossible. An unexpected burst of pleasure came over him, and he ejaculated inside Maria. He continued stroking, which didn't alert her that he had cum. His teeth sunk into her neck as he did his best to remain balanced. Maria kept her arms wrapped around Ramir's neck and her lips locked with his. Before she knew it, she had reached her peak again.

Ramir rolled out of Maria and also out the bed. He headed straight to the bathroom to clean up a bit. His rod was still semi-hard and could see why there was a sudden change during sex. The condom had broken. He removed the rubber ring from around his rod and flushed it down the toilet. *Fuck, I knew that shit was feeling too good. She is going to be pissed when she finds out I came in her.*

Ramir exited the bathroom and began gathering his clothes. "Damn you have a nice body," Maria said.

"You better stop, before I come over there for round two."

"Come here."

Ramir plopped on the bed. Maria handed him a glass of champagne and held hers in the air. "To new beginnings," she announced. Ramir raised his glass in the air for the cheers and then gulped down the beverage. Maria poured him another glass, which was also immediately gulped down.

"So let's talk about business," Ramir said.

"What do you want to talk about?"

"I want to know what needs to be done to get a better price on the work you are providing us. We have been very loyal to your father, and that should be rewarded."

"Loyalty is very important, especially when it comes to business."

"I agree." Both of them looked each other in the eye. They could see right through each other's bullshit.

"You know who you remind me of?"

"Who?" Ramir asked, expecting to be compared to someone great and powerful.

"Trey."

"Get the fuck outta' here. You better be talkin' bout Trey Songz."

"Eres gracioso," Maria said while chuckling. "You already know which Trey I'm talking about."

"Don't even mention that snitch's name in the same sentence as mine."

"Well, he was eager too. He came to me about expanding outside of Atlanta."

"Why the hell would he want to do that?"

"Why not?" she asked. "The Street Kings are strong enough to take over more than just Atlanta."

"But that would be too risky. We would have to deal with different police departments and not to mention beefing with other distributors."

"I understand what you're saying, but I believe it can be done."

"My father did it and look where he is now."

So many thoughts began running the Ramir's head. He was too focused on the D-Block gang's territory that he never thought about life outside of Atlanta. If he were able to get his feet set in North Carolina, he would be able to run an entire state, not just a block. Although a very tempting idea, this was something that he would need to run by Cash and get approval. That would mean dealing with the cartel directly.

"Shit, I feel weird," Ramir said as he began feeling lightheaded.

"You ok, Papi?"

"Yeah, I'm good. I just feel weird."

"Maybe you need some rest. You had a long drive down here twice already. Maybe your body is trying to tell you something."

Ramir sat back on the bed, in an attempt to get comfortable. His vision began blurring, and his responses were slow. Maria continued asking him questions but his speech was so slurred, she couldn't understand his responses. After about a minute, Ramir was knocked out cold. Maria grabbed her phone from the nightstand and quickly began pressing numbers before raising the phone to her ear to speak.

"Lo tengo."

# Chapter 34

"Tell me what your beef is with me," Ayanna barked, storming into the office.

"Sorry Sarge, I told her you were busy," one of the detectives said, grabbing Ayanna by the wrist.

"Get the fuck off of me!" she yelled, flaring her arms up in the air. Another detective came in to assist in removing Ayanna from the office.

"Let her be. It's ok," Sergeant Packard said, dismissing his subordinates.

Ayanna was pissed off. She flew into homicide headquarters like a bat out of hell. There was nothing to lose, and she was determined to get her answers. Without a badge or a gun, her career was over. "Tell me why you have been undermining my cases for all these years."

Sergeant Packard continued typing away at a report he was finishing up. Besides briefly looking over to see who had stormed into his office, his focus was on the computer screen. "What are you talking about young lady?" he asked without looking over at Ayanna.

"I know about the Corey King murder case. I know you were the one that handled the investigation."

"How do you know that?" he asked, perking up in his seat.

"I saw the case file. Did you even try to investigate the murder or did you have something to do with it?"

"First of all, I need you to close my door."

Ayanna looked back and realized people were ear hustling, trying to gather every single detail they could for the rumor mill. She slowly closed the door but immediately gave Sergeant Packard a sinister look, demanding her question be answered. He smiled, and then reached in the middle drawer of his desk.

"Here you go," he said, throwing her cell phone on the surface of the desk. "So do you really love him?" he asked as she reached down for the phone.

"What?"

"Do you really love him?"

It took a second for his question to register. She looked at her phone and realized why he was asking her that. *This motherfucker went through my shit.* "Didn't I tell you to get a damn warrant before going through my damn phone?"

He laughed. "Please tell me why you think I would take any orders from you?" He stood to his feet and looked at the broken woman that stood before him. "Do you really love him?"

"That's none of your fuckin' business."

"...and the Corey King file was none of yours."

"I was the first officer at the scene. I've never received an update on the case, and you never took a statement from me."

"Oh but I do have a statement from you," Sergeant Packard said while laughing.

"But I didn't make one."

"I know you didn't. I made it for you."

"So you created a false statement? Why?"

"I did it because I can. I didn't want anyone interfering with my case, not even a rookie that was still wet behind the ears."

"So what about that case made you put a target on my back? Every time I turn around, you are popping up at all of my crime scenes and stopping me from doing my job."

Sergeant Packard began pacing around the room. The sinister grin seemed to be glued to his face. "You know what I find funny? You came in here yelling and screaming about some old ass murder case, but not once did you ask about the current case in which you are a suspect. Tell me why."

Ayanna stayed silent and just watched Sergeant Packard pace back and forth. *He has been around long enough to know what happened.* In her opinion, his demeanor was strange. He was always aggressive and mean to her, but now he was calm and respectful. They were now caught up in a game of cat and mouse. They both had questions that needed to be answered, but no answers were being given. Ayanna didn't know how much longer she could keep up with the back and forth. She had to replay the past ten years back in her mind. *What the hell is his connection to me? Every time I get a lead on the Street Kings, he pops up—EVERY TIME.* "It's the Street Kings," she blurted aloud. She started jumping for joy.

"What?"

"It's not me. It's the Street Kings. This entire time, it seemed like you were after me, but you weren't. Every case you interfered with had something to do with the Street Kings. Whether it was Corey King's death or a homicide investigation involving Ace Newton, you were always there. What is your connection with them?"

"I can't answer any of your questions right now," he muttered, opening one of the drawers in his file cabinet. He removed a lock box and placed it on the desk. Placing his thumb on the digital scanner, he accessed the box. Ayanna leaned forward, peeking in the box, only to get a glimpse of large manila envelopes. "Everything you want to know is in this box. These files hold some of the darkest secrets that could cripple the entire Atlanta Police Department. One day I will let you look through these files to see why it was so important for me to shadow those cases."

He grabbed the top envelope and opened it. Four Polaroid photographs were taken out of the envelope and handed to Ayanna.

She looked at the photographs, noticing the same people in each one, three young boys and two men. One of the men was easily recognizable. He was standing right in front of her. The other was none other than *Corey King*. Ayanna looked up at Sergeant Packard and then back down at the photographs. She just happened to turn one over and see that someone had written on the back. ***COREY, JOE, JON, CHRIS, DON, 1997***. *Oh shit, he knows them.*

"What the hell is going on Sergeant?"

"I think its best that you give it all some time and it will come together. Do me a favor, when you talk to Don tell him Uncle Joe said hi."

# Chapter 35

Deuce sat in his car, looking at the news article. The massacre at The Cut was being talked about on every news station and in every magazine and newspaper. *Dismembered bodies left hanging on trees in neighborhood apartment,* the headline read. The brutality that went into the killings had the Street Kings written all over it. He only knew two men ruthless enough to kill someone in such a manner—Ace and Ramir. There was no limit to how far they would go to protect the organization. A part of Deuce wanted to compliment them on making a move that would be considered historical one day. The other part of him wondered what they did to his sister and nephews. There was no way they were going to let her walk away when she was labeled as an associate of a snitch.

"I miss you, Naomi," he whispered while scrolling through his cell phone, looking at her pictures.

He wiped a single tear from his face and put the phone down. He had lost everything; his family was gone and also his source of income. Deuce had been exiled from the organization. He hadn't heard from Ramir or Nate since the court hearing.

Lightning flashed across the sky, illuminating the dark street. Thunder crackled and echoed in the air. Deuce listened to the pitter-patter of the raindrops beating down on the Pontiac Grand Prix. He adjusted his seat to get comfortable. He had already been sitting at that location for a few hours and planned to continue sitting until it was time to make a move. The rain had been steady all day. The heavy downpour made it difficult to see out the windshield. Activating the windshield wipers could have compromised his position, so Deuce patiently waited to see a glare from headlights. There had been no activity since he parked up, but he had time to kill.

A black Glock .45 caliber handgun rested on the front passenger seat. It was in arm's reach just in case Deuce needed to handle any immediate problems. The rain picking up seemed to be an advantage for him. He was sure no one was out doing rounds in this type of weather. It would be a grave mistake if they were to be out checking the area and ran into him. Somebody was going to tell Deuce everything he wanted to know about the disappearance of his nephew and sister and until he got his answers bodies were going to drop. He didn't care if he had to kill every member of the Street Kings and anyone affiliated with them, he was determined to get the answers he wanted.

Hours were passing by, and the rain still hadn't let up. Deuce just got done filling up his fourth Gatorade bottle with piss. His eyes were bloodshot, and his eyelids were getting heavy. Fatigue was finally starting to kick in. He needed to get some rest. There was still no movement outside the gates of Cash's mansion, which seemed unusual. Cash was always in and out of the mansion, even when he was hosting parties and throwing cookouts. There was always a point where he headed out and handled business on the streets. Deuce had planned to confront the head honcho because if someone wanted to get rid of Naomi, that order would have to go through Cash for approval. It didn't seem like that day would be coming soon enough.

The fatigue finally got to Deuce, as his head began bopping up and down. His chin bounced off his chest and drool dripped out his mouth. The rain was starting to let up. The loud ringing of his phone immediately woke him from the unexpected slumber. He gathered his bearings before screening the call. *NO CALLER ID.* He declined the call and looked around. There was no movement outside the mansion. The sun began rising and Deuce decided to stay put, hoping to run into Cash. His phone began ringing again. *NO CALLER ID.* Once again, he declined the call. Seconds later the phone began ringing again. *NO CALLER ID.*

"Who the fuck is this?"

"Is this Mr. Ikawa?"

Deuce looked at the phone. *Who the fuck is calling me by my government name? Nobody ever uses my last name,* he thought. "Yo who is this?"

"This is Agent Miles from the Federal Bureau of Investigations."

"What the fuck do you want?"

"I want to talk to you about your sister, Naomi. Has your family heard from her yet?" Agent Miles asked.

"Heard from her? Listen man, we ain't gon' be hearing from her."

"Why do you say that?"

"You and I both know she ain't showing back up, so let's cut all this bullshit small talk, and get to the point. What the fuck do you want?"

"I want you to help me put the Street Kings behind bars."

"How the hell is that going to happen?"

"We want to know if you have any information that could help us. Anything you may know about their drug operations or the murders they were behind would help us tremendously."

"Why would I help y'all? I'm not a fuckin' rat."

"I know you want justice for your sister and so do we. We know they had something to do with her disappearance and we need you to help us make them pay for it."

Deuce stared at the front gate, still waiting for anyone to appear. The suspense was killing him. He was ready to just run up in the mansion and murk everybody inside. There was nothing the police or F.B.I. could do for him.

"Listen, I'm not helping the fuckin' Feds, so y'all might as well find somebody else. How the fuck did y'all even get my number?"

"We can get anyone's number. Just like we know exactly where anyone is located at any given time. How long before one of these guys come out and spots you?"

Deuce popped up in his seat and looked around. The same vehicles from the night prior were still on the street. There were three sedans, two SUVs and a minivan. One of the SUV's, an older model Nissan Pathfinder, flashed its headlights. "Are y'all following me?" he asked Agent Miles, nervous about the possibility of the Feds running up on him while he had his strap.

"I don't think that matters. All I'm going to say is you didn't do that good of a job at being discreet," Agent Miles responded. He and two other agents were on the block when Deuce pulled up. They watched him park close to the mansion and never exit his vehicle the entire night. They had cars drive by Deuce throughout the night. They ran his registration plate through the DMV database. Any move Deuce made would have been witnessed by agents and caught on video from their surveillance team.

Deuce quickly disconnected the call. Frustrated at the fact he was exposed, he shifted into gear and stomped on the gas pedal. With his tires screeching and transmission jerking into gear, the Pontiac made its way down the street. Deuce shoved his gun under his seat and repeatedly checked his rearview mirror, making sure he wasn't being followed. It was time to get back to the drawing board and find a new plan. With the Feds watching, he would need to be strategic if he wanted to get to Cash.

# Chapter 36

Cash and Ace stepped off the plane and were welcomed by the natives. Cash had been to Jamaica plenty of times, but each time the welcoming was always expected. People from the Caribbean were so polite, but it was something about Jamaicans that made you want to keep coming back to the island. The well-dressed men entered the airport and were immediately surrounded by taxi drivers and event planners that wanted to make some good money. They didn't know that there were already arrangements in place for the two Street Kings.

"Yo bredrin!" a man yelled out with a heavy accent.

Cash and Ace watched as everyone parted like the Red Sea as the man approached. Davinderjit aka Danja had a bold walk. He was a king amongst mere men. His long dreadlocks swung back and forth. His 6'4", 250-

pound frame was intimidating in itself. Danja was well known throughout the entire island. Cash knew him as Reana's older brother, but on the island he was a god. Everyone feared the Dread Headz and their leader was now strolling through the airport. Everyone was so focused on Danja that they didn't notice the two men that accompanied him. Their dreads were just as long as his and their hands were tucked under their shirts, a clear indication they were armed.

The on-duty Jamaican Police Officers had their blinders on. They knew a problem with the Dread Headz meant a death sentence. The island was small, and everyone knew everyone. A former captain on the police force had a vendetta against the Dread Headz. He believed the crime and problems they brought to the island was giving Jamaicans a bad name. One day the captain arrested Barrington "Banga" Roberts, who is not only Danja and Reana's little brother but he was also one of the heads of their crew. By that night, the captain received word that his home was torched and his entire family was killed in the blaze. Ever since that incident, the police have been hands off when it came to the Dread Headz.

"Danja, what up bro," Cash greeted. The men shook hands. "This is my boy Ace," Cash introduced. "Ace, this is Danja."

"What up bredda. Welcome to Jamrock," Danja greeted Ace.

"Thanks man, I'm happy to be here. I'm just ready to get some bomb ass weed."

Danja laughed. "Well yuh ave cum to di right place."

Cash and Ace headed to get their luggage and then headed outside. Danja was waiting outside, standing between two white Mercedes Benz G550s. Airport personnel loaded the luggage into the SUVs, and the men headed toward Kingston. The SUVs cruised down the dirt roads back to back. This was the strategy of the Dread Headz. They always traveled in pairs and drove identical cars. Although they were powerful, they weren't invincible. Several rival gangs have tried to take their spot at the top. They launched attacks on the crew, which led to violence spreading throughout the island. The Dread Headz took no prisoners. They burned people alive, including elders and children. The Dread Headz didn't have to worry about local authorities like the Street Kings had to worry about Atlanta Police, so there was no limit to their ruthlessness. If you attacked them, they went after your entire family. Their violence made the attack on the D-Block gang look like an insignificant punishment. Ace was stuck looking out the window, taking in the island's beauty. He still was trying to adjust to being on the opposite side of the road. He laughed at the goats and horses that were tied up to poles and left on the side of the road. Jamaica was so different from Atlanta.

The three-hour ride from the airport to Kingston, allowed the visitors to see a lot of the island. They saw beautiful homes and unique structures, but they also saw people outside metal shacks. Jamaica was no different from any other place. There was poverty but there was also luxury.

As they entered Kingston and drove through town, everyone's head turned as each of the Mercedes SUVs drove by. Kids ran up to the SUVs, begging for money. Danja had the drivers slow down as they threw money at the kids. He remembered being one of those kids back in the day, not knowing when his next meal would come. Although he was ruthless, he was also compassionate. He protected his people, especially those that lived in Kingston. He was disgusted at the gentrification that was taking place on the island. Foreigners were coming in, buying up property, opening businesses, and were getting rich on the backs of the locals. To them, Jamaicans were just cheap labor. They knew the island was stricken with poverty and that people would be in dire need of some form of income. Danja planned on reviving the island and allowing his people to become more independent. He had a vision of Jamaican-owned business popping up and being successful beyond anyone's wildest dreams. He envisioned foreigners coming to the island and only being able to work for Jamaican businesses. They would no longer be able to profit off his homeland.

The Dread Headz had already begun extorting the foreign business owners, forcing them to fork over a percentage of their income each month. This money was used to build homes throughout Kingston and to start a large marijuana grow operation. The herb was grown throughout the island, but Danja and Reana wanted to start exporting it to other countries. This operation would solidify their wealth and allow them to rebuild the broken communities. Cash and Ace were there to help them with the plan.

The SUVs slowed down, and both men looked out the window at the pink mansion they were approaching. They stopped at the front gate, where young Jamaicans surrounded the SUVs. Cash and Ace both noticed that the young men were armed with a variety of handguns, rifles, and machetes. As soon as they noticed Danja was in the front SUV, they backed up and one of the men signaled up for the gates to be open.

"Damn y'all ain't playing around here," Ace said.

"Di kingdom muss always be protected," Danja shot back.

Pulling up the long driveway, Cash and Ace looked up at the mansion. It was big, but the exterior wasn't as luxurious as Cash's mansion in Atlanta. He wasn't big on the different tones that were used either. The exterior walls were a light pink, and the roof was a darker tone. Some of the walls were cracked and chipped away. The balconies were painted an off-white and riflemen stood on each balcony, looking down at the arriving vehicles.

"Security is tight around here," Cash said.

"Indeed," Danja replied.

"That's good though. That allows you to sleep peacefully at night."

"Me?" Danja laughed. "Mi nuh live inna fuckin pink yaad. Dis a weh yuh empress lives."

"Reana lives in this big mansion by herself?'

"Yah mon."

Cash laughed because Reana would always complain about how big his mansion was for just the two of them. The last time he visited, she had a nice little spot in Montego Bay where they stayed and now she had completely upgraded. The SUVs stopped at the front door, and the men exited. The front doors of the mansion opened, and Reana and Banga walked out. She looked like a true goddess. Her dreads were pulled up in a bun, the rays from the sun bounced off her glowing skin, and the Versace bikini top and skirt fit snug on her amazing body. Cash wanted to run up and tongue down his woman, but he knew her brother wouldn't want to see that much affection being displayed. He walked up the steps and gave her a tight hug, followed up by a quick peck on her lips. Next, he greeted Banga with a handshake hug. "Thank you for everything," Cash said to the man behind the killings of Los and Willis Jamison. Banga and his small crew enjoyed the work they were able to put in during their time in Atlanta.

"Mi fos time visiting di states an mi did able to capture sum souls," Banga muttered as he caressed the forty caliber handgun that was tucked in his shorts. Banga was known as the Jamaican Reaper. He made Ace and Ramir look like amateurs. He loved to kill and enjoyed it more than he enjoyed sex. Banga caught his first body at twelve years old when he stabbed a schoolmate over a comment that was made about Reana. A rumor went around school about Reana being fast and before the day ended, Banga found out who started the rumor. The boy was found in the bathroom with a small dagger in the side of his neck. After that day, Banga's craving for souls grew. When he was eighteen years old, the Dread Headz gang was officially started, and he helped give them their violent reputation as he publicly butchered rivals.

"Ok, let's head out back to chat bizniz," Reana said knowing her brothers were eager to increase their income.

When the Dread Headz began their gang, the primary source of income was from marijuana sells. Although they did well in the beginning, it was hard to profit off a product that anyone on the island could produce. As they grew in size, the marijuana income wasn't enough to ensure everyone was comfortable. This problem caused a lot of tension between members of the gang, and things began heading in a negative direction. To increase income, they decided to get involved with armed robberies. In the beginning, they robbed other gangs and drug dealers, but then they began focusing on businesses. The robberies led to shootings, which led to murders, which led to wars taking place on the island. When there is war, there are casualties. Drive-by shootings took the lives of innocent people, and that didn't sit right with Danja. At the time, he was second in command behind Badrick "Bossman" Beckford.

Bossman was on a destructive path that would have led to the death of hundreds or even thousands of innocent people. Danja loved his island and people too much to allow this to go on. He suggested robbing tourists, which not only produced more quality acquisitions but also decreased killings on the island. Word of the robberies got out, and travelers began to use caution. They stopped going on excursions and visiting towns outside of resorts. This led to the desperate move of sneaking into resorts to find victims. Bossman often went and took Reana along with him. The tactic was successful but didn't produce enough income to feed the entire gang. Only the top members were able to live comfortably. The resorts ended up bumping up security, which made it difficult for them to get into the resorts. Danja hated the idea of his sister going on these missions, which is why when Bossman was killed during one of the missions, Danja couldn't wait to step up as the head of the Dread Headz.

His priority was to go after the foreigners he felt were extorting his island, and that's exactly what he did. Although things had been going well for the Dread Headz, Danja wanted to step in front of any further issues before they became problems. He knew the income they were bringing in would not be enough to assist in his dreams. They had to find another source of income before it was too late.

Everyone headed to the back of the mansion where a DJ was playing music, and a beautiful bartender was mixing drinks. Gorgeous Jamaican women of all shades and sizes filled the pool. All eyes were on Ace and Cash. Their swag immediately stood out. Reana wrapped her arms around Cash and gave him a passionate kiss, and then shot a deadly look at every woman in the pool. They all looked away, knowing she just claimed her territory. Danja laughed after seeing the slick move his sister just pulled.

"Listen man, I'm 'bout to go for a swim. Y'all getting' in or nah?" Ace asked.

"Naw, go ahead," Cash said. "I'll be over here if you need me."

Ace wasted no time stripping down to his boxers and diving into the pool. Like a bloody carcass in a pool full of piranhas, Ace was fresh meat, and the women circled him before going in for the kill. These women envied Reana. They saw the designer clothes she wore, the fancy jewelry she showed off, and the power she had over men. They wanted that and at that moment, Ace

271

was their key to that type of lifestyle. In their eyes, he was a meal ticket. Ace was used to this type of attention, but not their aggression. Hands were rubbing his chest, back, neck, and every other area on his body. Banga and Danja both looked at the desperate women in disgust.

"Jamaicans should ave more pride bredda," Banga muttered.

"Soon dem wi bredda. Soon dem wi," Danja responded.

"Ok, so let's get straight to business," Cash said as he sat down at the table that was set up for their meeting.

Reana's cooks prepared a delicious spread that included curry chick, roti, patties, raisin slices, fresh fruit, and fresh-squeezed juice. There were also bottles of rum cream on the table. Cash grabbed a mango and bit into the sweet fruit. Reana and her brothers sat down as well.

"Where's my suitcase?" Cash asked, wiping his mouth with a napkin.

Danja called for one of his men to bring their belongings over. The young Jamaican sprinted to the SUVs and brought the large suitcases to the rear of the house. Cash grabbed his suitcase and unzipped it. He removed a large duffle bag and placed it on the table.

"I'm sorry that y'all had to leave Atlanta in such a hurry, but this is for the work you put in for me and my team. I usually pay up front, so I put a little extra in there for the wait."

Reana grabbed the bag and looked inside. Her eyes lit up, and she immediately looked over at her brothers and handed them the bag. Danja and Banga both looked in the bag. "Bumboclaat dis a nuff funds," Danja broadcasted as he popped shots from his gun, in the air.

*BANG! BANG! BANG! BANG! BANG!*

The women and the pool flinched and looked to see why shots are being fired. Ace even looked, subconsciously reaching in his waistband, forgetting he was in the pool. "Dis funds a guh feed nuff families."

Cash was happy that Danja was happy about the payment, but couldn't understand the extreme reaction. He looked over at Reana, and she smiled back at him. He knew her too well to see past the smile. "Is everything ok here?" Cash asked.

"No wi ave been struggling bredrin. Fi wi crew needs more of dis," Danja said, holding up the duffle bag.

"Why is the first I'm hearing 'bout this?" Cash asked Reana. She knew he would do anything for her and her brothers, especially after securing their freedom.

"Mi neva tell yuh cuz yuh had nuff gwaan. Yuh neva need more problems pan yuh plate," she replied.

"Baby, your problems are my problems. So what is the problem?"

"There no funds coming inna. Barely any funds coming inna from di tourists an di ganja sales horrible. Fi wi crew hungry an dem need fi be able to feed dem families."

"Yeah, I know what you mean. The wolves only stay in the pack if their leader makes sure they eat. Shit, sometimes when they are eating, they still leave. Just like Trey."

Reana nodded in agreement. Her one fear was having members of her crew turn on them. She already had one of their top hitmen's hands chopped off because he was skimming off the top of the money he was collecting from the foreign businesses. He did it because he needed more money for his family. He didn't get into the street life to be making minimum wage, but unfortunately, he had to be punished for his disloyalty. After having his hands chopped off, Reana exiled him from Kingston, and they haven't heard from him since.

"Tell him about ganja man," Danja chimed in.

"Who the fuck is ganja man?"

"Sum old man dat tip wi off bout a snake inna di crew. Di old man claim him overheard a conversation di man did having inna bar bout stealing from wi. Wi confirmed dat di information did true," Reana said.

"So why do y'all call him ganja man?"

"Cuz him keeps chatting Danja bout shipping ganja ova to di states. Him say wi cya get rich but wi nuh kno weh to start.

"That makes sense. Then you wouldn't have to compete with everyone who is growing and selling. If you really want to make money, y'all can have your crew move some coke too."

"Mi nuh wa dat crap flooding Jamaica!" Danja barked while slamming his gun on the table. "Mi wa fi empowa Jamaicans nuh mek dem drug addicts."

"Then don't sell to Jamaicans. Sell to the tourists. They are going to pay top dollar and your crew will make twice as much money than they would with weed."

"Dat a true bredrin. But ow wi a guh get cocaine?"

Cash chuckled. "Well since you are going to be opening an import and export business; you will be importing cocaine and exporting marijuana. I will supply you with the cocaine, so don't worry about that end of things. The only thing you need to focus on is making sure your crew is loyal and finding a bigger bank because the money is going to be rolling in."

"Yuh a fuckin' genius," Danja shouted. BANG! BANG! BANG! He let off more shots in the air. Cash's suggestion was exactly what he wanted to hear. There would be no question that their crew would not only be powerful but also wealthy. They would no longer need to tax the foreign businesses because they would be able to shut them down completely. The Dread Headz were ready to rebuild Kingston and Jamaica."

"Oh yeah, Ganja man also tell wi to open nightclubs. Him say di resorts wi bring tourists to wi instead of wi a guh dem," Reana told Cash.

"That makes sense. Not just nightclubs though. You can open restaurants, villas, and shopping centers. You could let these jobs help your people, and your crew can move the work when the tourists come through. Then you won't have to worry about any issues with resort security or the cops. You will make millions. All of you."

"Wi a guh need help. Wi need sum'ady dat cya run it all fi wi."

"I think I have the perfect person," Cash said while smiling.

"Who?"

"Mir," he replied.

"Ramir?" Reana asked. There was excitement in her voice. She witnessed how Ramir ran the organization when Cash was locked up, so she knew he would surely take the Dread Headz to the next level. "Ramir a guh luv it here."

Cash couldn't wait to get back and tell Ramir the good news. He would no longer have to just be a hitta' for the organization. He would now be running his own organization. He wouldn't even have to move to Jamaica. He could pop in every month to ensure everything was going as planned. Reana, Danja, and Banga would still run their crew, and they would make Ramir filthy rich. Working alongside the Dread Headz would be a reward for his loyalty. It would also be a consistent form of income for the Street Kings as the distributor.

"Yo Ace, you think Ramir would like expanding our reach to Jamaica?"

"Man, he gon' love this shit!" Ace yelled out as the women continued seducing him. Ace knew the hard work Ramir put in and appreciated it. His little cousin deserved what he was about to get.

... TO BE

CONTINUED

# BE ON THE LOOKOUT FOR THE NEXT BOOKS IN THIS SERIES

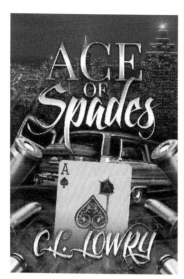

# BONUS Chapter

The door to the large storage locker was pulled up, and a dim light was on in the corner. Nicolás Muñoz entered the locker and closed the door behind him. He was dressed in a tan Kiton suit, white dress shirt, and Mezlan crocodile shoes. The odor of bloody flesh filled the small area. Nicolás removed his suit jacket and draped it over a chair that in the corner of the room. The odor bounced around Nicolás' nostrils. The scent was intoxicating to him. Nicolás loosened his tie and rolled up the sleeves of his dress shirt. He walked toward the center of the storage locker, toward a naked man that was curled up in the fetal position on the ground. The man was lying in a pool of his blood. Deep lacerations covered his face and body. Four men stood in each corner of the storage locker, each of them in possession of machetes.

"El hijo de puta," Nicolás muttered before spitting on the man. He hovered around, circling the man like a vulture in the sky. "Esto es lo que hacemos a las serpientes," he announced proudly.

Although the sight before him pleased his dark soul, he wasn't happy about the reason behind the man's unforeseen fate. Treachery had reared its ugly head.

Nicolás grabbed a crate from the corner of the storage locker and placed it just above the male's head, before sitting on it. His heartbeat was steady, his palms were dry, and there was no expression on his face. He felt betrayed but didn't show it. The man that he rested his eyes on was once considered an ally, and now it was time to cut all ties with the traitor.

"I guess you didn't think we were going to find out," Nicolás whispered into one of the bloody ears before pulling out a stack of papers that he had rolled up in his back pocket. He threw the papers down at his feet, just in the line of sight of the man's swollen eyes.

"You know what this is? These are the cell phone records from my sons, from the week they went missing. Guess who was the last person they contacted?" There was no response except groans as the pain from the man's wounds began to worsen. "You were texting and calling Alejandro on the same night that I last heard from him. Did you kill my sons, la perra?"

"I di—didn't do this."

*SMACK!*

"Cállate," Nicolás growled after backhanding the man in the face. "Don't you fuckin' lie to me!" Nicolás closed his eyes for a brief moment. He couldn't help but think about his boys. "Do you know how hard I tried to keep my boys away from this lifestyle? I also tried to keep my daughter away, but they all want to be a part of all of this craziness. My boys didn't find out what I did for a living until they were teenagers. As soon as they found out what I was involved in, they immediately wanted to sell drugs. Do you believe that? They were rich and they aspired to be corner boys. My biggest mistake was raising them in America and not Colombia. They were fascinated with all this Hollywood bullshit. They wanted fame over money, and that is dangerous. They wanted to be known. It is better to move in silence because the more noise you make, the more trouble you invite into your world; trouble like you. I allowed them to be distributors so they would be safe. I thought I could keep them safe. Tell me what you did with my sons."

"I didn't —"

*SMACK!*

Nicolás backhanded Ramir in the face a second time. The lion's head ring he was wearing left a bloody imprint on Ramir's cheek.

Nicolás reached into his pocket and pulled out a tool. He grabbed Ramir's left hand and positioned his pinky finger between the blades of the pruning shears. Nicolás expected Ramir to begin begging at this point, but the young street soldier was molded to withstand his current situation. Nicolás slowly squeezed the handle of the shears, watching the blades slice into the finger.

"ARRRRGGGHHH!" Ramir screamed at the top of his lungs as Nicolás began to dismember his hand. One by one, Nicolás took away the fingers off both hands. Ramir's screams sent a chill down Nicolás' neck. The young soldier began to fade in and out. He was losing too much blood.

"Uhhh. Th—they weren't who you think they were." Ramir spit out a large glob of blood.

His body ached, and each laceration burned to his core. A stabbing pain in his torso left him balled up on the ground, as a result of several broken ribs. He was so weak and battered; he could barely lift his head to look at Nicolás. The swelling around his eyes blinded him, and the blood that filled his broken nose made it nearly impossible to breathe. This had been the first time Ramir was ever in this type of position. He had always been a hunter, and now he had become the hunted. Even after covering their tracks by disposing of the bodies, cell phones, and vehicles of the Muñoz brothers after killing them, Ramir made one grave mistake. He called them from a traceable number that came back to him, so once Nicolás pulled the phone records, he was able to put the pieces of the puzzle together.

"Where are my sons? Are they alive?"

Ramir coughed up another glob of blood. "I don't know."

"Stop lying. Did your bosses make you do this? Did Cristóbal give you the orders to kill my sons?"

Ramir gathered the last bit of energy he had left. "Fuck you."

Nicolás thought long and hard about anyone who could have been involved in the disappearance of his sons. The Street Kings were the last crew he expected to betray him, especially because the crew was making so much money off his product. There was so much disbelief. Cash even agreed to assist him in the search for his sons. However, since he felt as though The Street Kings had betrayed him, he was ready to send a message. Nicolás grabbed one of the machetes from his henchmen. "Soy el rey de las calles." With one fell swoop, Ramir's head rolled a foot away from his body.

"I'M THE KING OF THE STREETS"

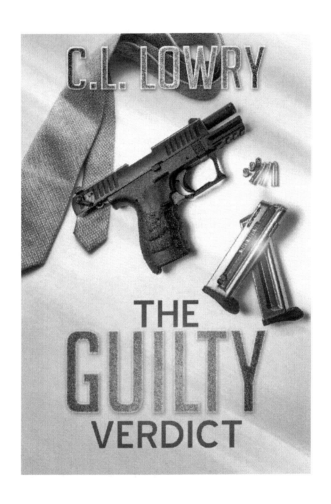

# Also Available from C.L. Lowry

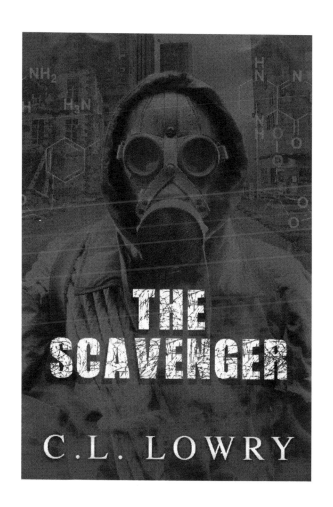

# Also Available from C.L. Lowry

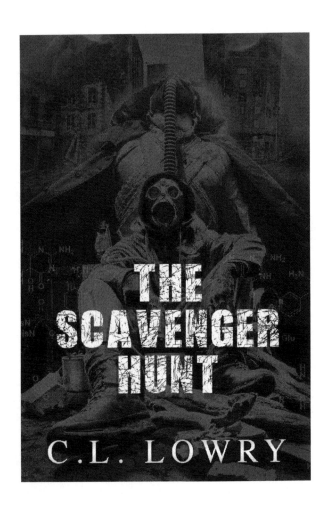

# Coming Soon from C.L.Lowry

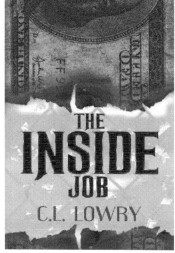

# About the Author

**C.L. Lowry** is an award-winning author and filmmaker. Although he prides himself as being a prolific crime novelist, his pen game is versatile and allows him to navigate through multiple genres. Lowry was born and raised in Philadelphia, Pennsylvania but his family roots trace back to the beautiful island of Barbados, West Indies. Lowry uses his life experiences and creativity to demand his readers' attention with realistic scenarios throughout his stories.

When he isn't penning a page-turning novel, Lowry is behind the camera creating high-quality films under his production company, Black Lens Cinema. Lowry is also the host of the Fiction Addiction Podcast, where he interviews authors, filmmakers, and other creatives. Sign up for Lowry's spam-free newsletter to learn more about future releases, sneak peeks, special offers, and bonus content. Subscribers will also receive access to exclusive giveaways. To sign up, visit his website at www.authorcllowry.com.

# Creedom Publishing Company

Creedom Publishing is a fully incorporated publishing company. Much like our slogan "The Home of Creative Freedom," we are committed to providing new and upcoming authors with the resources and opportunity to share their *creativity* with the world. At Creedom Publishing, writers have the *freedom* to make their own choices, without the burden of committing to one-sided contracts and guidelines that most traditional publishing companies offer. We are located in the Philadelphia area of Pennsylvania.

**Our books are available for purchase on our site and eBooks are available through Amazon Kindle.**

CONTACT THE CREEDOM PUBLISHING COMPANY AT:

CREEDOMPUBLISHING@OUTLOOK.COM

OR BY MAIL AT:

CREEDOM PUBLISHING COMPANY
P.O. BOX 683
Gilbertsville, PA 19525

Made in the USA
Columbia, SC
21 July 2024

39125121R00176